THE RUNAWAY

Erick Livumbazi Ngoda

Worlds Unknown Publishers

ISBN: 978-1-7343917-0-1 (Paperback)
ISBN: 978-1-7343917-6-3 (Hardcover)
ISBN: 978-1-7343917-7-0 (Ebook)

Printed in the United States of America.
First printing edition 2019.

Worlds Unknown Publishers
2515 E Thomas Rd,
Ste 16 -1061
Phoenix, AZ 85016-7946

www.wupubs.com

Keep safe. When in doubt, be slow to trust.

Contents

GETTING THE SPICES

"Oh no! I've forgotten to pick up the spices from Zaruni's shop!" Ma Rahma, Ahmed's mum, sighed. The spices were for her cousin Zaruni's wedding. Ma Rahma was going to do most of the cooking.

"Why don't you leave some of those things for the others to deal with?" Ahmed's dad grunted from behind the newspaper he was reading.

"Everyone else is helping. I'm not the only one doing things. Everyone is helping with this wedding," Biti Rahma said, spreading out her palms and nodding her head firmly for emphasis. Ahmed often called his mother Ma Rahma like everyone else, not Mum the way most of the other children called their mothers. She always wanted to do a lot of things at the same time. She often took up most of the work that she could have shared with other people.

As soon as she talked about the forgotten spices, Ahmed knew straight away that he was going to be sent to the store to get them. It was during the school holidays; the afternoon seemed hotter than most others. He was lying drowsily on a *mkeka* under the shade of the leafy mango tree in a corner of the compound, dozing off and waking up from time to time in the intense afternoon heat. He was planning to go over to his friend Ali's to play some PlayStation games. He had heard that Ali had the latest games—*Slay the Empire* and *Void Bastards*. He was dying to lay his hands on those. His younger sisters, Suya and Sabrina, were playing with their dolls near the outdoor kitchen.

"Ahmed!" Ma Rahma called out after a while.

"I'm right here . . . not in Saudi Arabia," Ahmed grumbled as he shuffled into the house.

"It's just one more errand I need you to run for me. No need to pull faces dear," Ma Rahma said as she firmly took him by his arm and led him back outside. She glanced over her shoulder to make sure that his dad could not hear her, and then whispered into Ahmed's ear, "I also forgot to pick up the women's *sarees* for the wedding. After you have picked up the spices from Zaruni's, go to Fundi Ghulam and give him this money." She pressed a roll of notes into Ahmed's palm. "He has a bag he can put them in for you . . . run! I will make you those nice *mahamri* when you come back . . . with cinnamon." She knew that she had him there. Ahmed really loved those spicy buns, and his mum made them the way no one else could. She practically pushed Ahmed out of the gate as soon as he tried to wiggle some more favors from her in return for the errand.

"Oh, dear," he mumbled to himself, shuffling his feet as soon as he was out of the gate.

The weekend was turning out to be one of the worst he could ever remember. It was better when he had to go to school. During the holidays, all there was to do was to be sent from place to place by his parents. He was not allowed to go out and play until all the chores were done. He couldn't even watch television until late in the evening when his father was home. It was better with Ma Rahma; he could always convince her to let him watch TV when he had done all the chores and run the errands.

"Amedoooo!" someone called out from the shops across the road, "I see you!" The voice was unmistakably that of Samir, his classmate from school. Ahmed saw him getting up from the chair on the verandah of the *duka* on which he had been sitting and started to walk over in his springy walk.

"Saidi just won twenty-five thousand shillings on Sportbet," Samir said excitedly. "They are going to have a party." He glanced over his shoulder exactly the way Ahmed's mother had done a few minutes ago. Sportbet is a betting company; through it, one could bet on the outcome of soccer games, mostly in the premier league. Ahmed was still feeling low. He couldn't share Samir's excitement.

"What is that you are holding in your hand? Money?" Samir asked his voice low but with a different kind of excitement. Ahmed quickly stuffed the wad of notes into his back pocket. He had not noticed that he had been holding them in his hand.

"Hey, that is a whole lot of money!" Samir pressed on.

"Leave me alone, will you? What is wrong with you?" Ahmed said irritably, clicking his tongue with annoyance.

"What is the money for? Please, please tell me!" Samir was not put off by his friend's cold response.

"I am running an errand for my mum," Ahmed answered just to get Samir off his case.

"Where?" Samir persisted, "with such a lot of money?"

"I'm going to pick up the women's sarees for Zaruni's wedding, okay?" Ahmed thought explaining everything would throw Samir off his back. But to his surprise, Samir excitedly clutched at the sleeve of his shirt and drew him to the side of the road.

"Look," he whispered after glancing furtively around, "we could make some money of our own from that." His breath was stale, and Ahmed quickly turned away from him.

"Mmmpphhh!" Ahmed made a face. "You are crazy. I have to pick up the sarees for Biti Rahma quickly. The women will be coming for them in the evening." He tried to pull his sleeve away from Samir's firm grip.

"Look here, there is still a lot of time. It's just two o'clock. Let's give Zuberi that money to bet for us. We could win a million shillings!"

Ahmed looked at his friend's face with alarm. "What have you been smoking?" he asked "You had better go somewhere and sleep it off, okay? Let me go where I have been sent. I have other things to do."

"Listen . . . *listen*," Samir persisted, "haven't you heard of Sportbet? You correctly predict the soccer teams that will win certain matches and you win a lot of money!

"Saidi just bet two hundred shillings, and he won twenty-five thousand shillings! Just think of how much you could win, with all that money in your pocket," Samir continued excitedly. Ahmed stopped and thought for a moment. He had heard of Sportbet. A lot of the men on their street often bet and sometimes he heard that someone had won a lot of money. He had not been paying much attention when Samir told him about it earlier, but he was all ears now.

"You will have your mother's money back and we will have much more to use as we want!"

Ahmed tried to brush away Samir's words, but they kept coming back into his head. They were making a lot of sense to him. Perhaps because the heat had cooked his brain or something.

Would he be able to buy a shiny fast car that he'd seen at the motor dealer in town? Would he be able to stroll into one of the big restaurants where the tourists went and order some of that expensive food that he sometimes saw when he passed by them? Everything he had ever dreamt of would be in the palm of his hand—designer clothes, exotic trips, hot girls. He would even be able to study privately and not go to school every day. Life would just be one big holiday!

"Hey, are you dreaming while awake?" Samir interrupted his thoughts.

"Errmm . . . huh!?" Ahmed grunted.

"So?" Samir asked anxiously, his hand still grasping Ahmed's sleeve.

"Let go of my sleeve!" Ahmed hissed, drawing away sharply. Samir quickly obeyed, not wanting to make his friend refuse to go along with his plan.

"Well," he persisted, "should we go ahead with it or what?"

"I don't know how to." Ahmed said uncertainly.

"That is why Zuberi will help us bet . . . see?" Samir spread out his hands as if there was nothing at all to the entire matter.

"If this goes wrong, it will all be your fault!" Ahmed grasped the front of Samir's shirt and made his voice as threatening as he could. Samir was a bit smaller than him, although they were both seventeen. Samir was always coming up with all sorts of ideas and schemes that often got them into trouble. Ahmed could never shake him off. A number of times, his parents had warned him to keep away from Samir. The only problem was that Samir wouldn't keep away from him.

"Nothing will go wrong . . . this time." Samir gulped before adding the last part, probably remembering the other times he had got his friend into trouble.

"Yeah!" You always say that, but you just wait until something happens. You know what plucked out the—" Ahmed started.

"Yes, the guinea fowl's head feathers." Samir rolled his eyes as he finished his friend's sentence for him. He had heard the same threat from Ahmed quite a number of times. But he hadn't yet found out what caused the bird's baldness.

"Samir, I mean it this time. I don't even see why I'm . . ." Ahmed made as if to walk away.

"No, listen!" Samir pleaded, clutching Ahmed's sleeve once again.

"Okay, let go!" Ahmed hissed and forcefully drew away his sleeve. The fact was that he was very interested in his friend's plan. But deep down inside, he was afraid of what could happen. Suppose he lost all the money? But there was no way he could lose it all, he reasoned. The men on his street bet so little money, and yet they won so much! There was no way it was going to go wrong. Plus, he was going to watch everything carefully. He was not going to let Samir trick him.

"But Samir, I swear, if I lose this money!" He knew very well that he was making the decision himself, but he wanted the blame to be totally on Samir, just in case.

"You . . . *we* will not lose it, I promise!" Samir smoothly affirmed. Ahmed didn't like the *we*. Was Samir going to claim half the money he was going to win? But he let it go. He was going to win the money first, then decide what to give Samir. After all, he was the stronger one.

They strolled over to the verandah where Zuberi and his friends were sitting. As soon as they were a few meters away, Samir signaled to Zuberi, who swiftly stood up and walked over.

THE ODDS

Y ou can bet on ongoing matches," Zuberi confided in a whisper. "In just a few minutes like this, wham, you can be a millionaire." Samir was literally dancing from one foot to another with excitement.

"But what if I lose all the money. It is my mother's." Ahmed didn't like the whiny sound in his voice, but he had to ask. Deep down inside him, he was still a bit worried.

"You will not lose the money. I know these things, Little Master. Aren't you the son of Ma Rahma?" Zuberi asked, putting his hand on Ahmed's shoulder and looking earnestly into his eyes.

"Ye . . . yes." Ahmed gulped some saliva nervously.

"You see!" Zuberi exclaimed, slapping Ahmed so sharply on one shoulder that he startled him.

"Ma Rahma is my very own sister! Why would I lie to my very, very own nephew?"

Ahmed felt a wave of reassurance, although it was the first time

he heard that Zuberi was his uncle. He hardly knew him! But if Zuberi was indeed his uncle, then everything was safe. Zuberi was a grown-up in a *kanzu*, straight from the mosque, apparently. Surely, there was no way that he could ever trick him! But there still was a strange kind of excitement that Zuberi had which made Ahmed a bit suspicious. Besides, Ahmed was a bit worried about the way Zuberi seemed to communicate with Samir without using words. It was like they had a plan that was known to just the two of them. But when he thought of all the things he could do with millions of shillings, everything else just flew out of his mind. That included the amount of talking to he was going to get from his father and just how much Ma Rahma was going to be upset. He really was going to get it from both sides if anything went wrong with the money; but nothing was going to go wrong, he was sure.

"The thing about life, son," Zuberi patted Ahmed's shoulder as he said in low, very wise sounding tones, "is that you have to think ahead and take risks. Fear will not take you anywhere. If Saidi had thought too much about how hungry his children were—how they would weep from hunger if he lost those two hundred shillings—would he be celebrating and have so much money now?"

He did not wait for Ahmed to answer, because it was a question that did not require an answer. Ahmed slipped his hand into his back pocket and slowly removed the wad of notes. Zuberi reached out and grabbed the money from him a bit too quickly for his liking. Ahmed also noticed that the hand with which Zuberi had taken the money was shaking a little. A cloud of worry drifted across his mind, but the sunshine of the possibilities ahead quickly drove it away.

"How much do we have here?" Zuberi asked. His voice had changed. Gone was the soft, convincing, cajoling tone. He suddenly sounded a bit rough and eager.

"Six thousand," Ahmed said hesitantly. It suddenly occurred to him that he should have given Zuberi only part of the money so as to stay on the safe side. But Zuberi was already moving back to the verandah where his friends were. He went through the doorway and into the shop. He had not even asked Ahmed and Samir to go along.

"Shouldn't we . . . follow him?" Ahmed asked Samir after a short awkward silence.

"Don't you trust him? He said he is your uncle." Samir shrugged, looking straight back at Ahmed.

"What? It was all your idea!" Ahmed made as if he was going to grab Samir's shoulder, but his friend ducked and moved away as if distancing himself from any trouble there was. It was very clear that Samir was putting himself in a midway place, where he was going to quickly impose himself into the winnings, if there was going to be any, and to duck and disassociate himself from the whole thing if it did not turn out as well as they hoped.

"What are you worrying about? The money will soon be here!" Samir said from one side of his mouth. Ahmed noticed the change in his attitude. It looked as if as soon as you handed over money, people's attitude changed. All the begging and pleading and treating you special stopped.

"Okay, should we follow him inside?" Ahmed asked anxiously. "He will soon be out. He has gone to check that book in which he writes the odds," Samir said smugly.

"Where he writes the *what*?" Ahmed asked.

"Odds . . . the chances a team has of sco—" Samir started to explain.

"Oh, whatever," Ahmed interrupted, not wanting his friend to enjoy the fact that he knew more than him. After a few minutes, Ahmed started getting a little worried. How long exactly was it going to take Zuberi to check the . . . whatever Samir had called them? He shifted his weight nervously. On the one hand, he wanted to find out exactly how long it was going to take for Zuberi to bet and before the millions arrived, but on the other hand, he did not want everyone, especially Samir, to know that he knew nothing at all about gaming and betting.

He thought it would take just a few minutes for the money he won to be sent. He was sure he was going to be a millionaire in the next few minutes. He was also blissfully unaware that he stood a greater chance of losing than winning. He squatted on the ground because he was so tired. Then he stood up again, walked around in a circle, and kicked up small puffs of dust. He looked up to the top of the coconut trees that were gently swaying in the afternoon breeze. Exactly how long was Zuberi going to take? He wished he had followed him inside the *duka*.

Samir was chatting away, talking about all the people that had won some money on Sportbet. They had not won much, because their bets had been small, or so he reasoned. But Ahmed was hardly listening. As more minutes, then close to an hour passed by, Samir started getting restless, and Ahmed became very worried. The money was taking so long to arrive! Had Zuberi checked the odds? Ahmed couldn't even remember whether he said orders because he was not conversant with betting.

"I want to go home. There is stuff I promised to do for my mum," Samir said uneasily.

"What!" Ahmed grabbed the front of Samir's shirt. "You are going to wait here with me!" he said forcefully, while gritting his teeth.

"Hey! Kids! Go and fight somewhere else!" one of the men on the verandah called out. The other two loudly agreed with him. Ahmed was so startled that he loosened his hold on Samir's shirt. Samir used the opportunity to wrench himself from Ahmed's grip and run off very fast between the vendors' stalls, along the street.

Ahmed felt the tears start to prick the back of his eyelids. He just wanted to sit down and weep. He was now so scared because he was all alone. What on earth was keeping Zuberi inside the shop? He decided to move closer to the men and ask them. He timidly approached them until he was a couple of meters away from them. "*Shikamoo*," he greeted them humbly, bowing slightly and bringing his hands together.

"*Marahaba!*" two of them replied, but the other one just stared at him.

"Please have you seen my . . . my uncle . . . Zuberi?' he asked timidly. Calling Zuberi his uncle felt a bit awkward. After all he had only discovered that day that they were related.

"Aren't you Ma Rahma's son?" one of the men asked after they had glanced knowingly at each other. Ahmed eagerly nodded his head. They knew him after all! They were going to help him. Everything was okay.

"How exactly is Zuberi your uncle? Your mother's or father's brother?" one of the two that hadn't returned his greeting asked.

"He . . . he said . . ." Ahmed stammered.

"Was he trying to get money from you?" the other one asked. "He . . . he said he was going to bet for me. He entered this *duka*." Ahmed suddenly started feeling quite stupid under their stares. "So, all the time you were standing over there with that other boy, you were waiting for him to bring back your money?" the man asked. Ahmed noticed that one of the others was trying to hide the fact that he was laughing behind his hand.

"He said he was going to check the . . . the orders for me." Ahmed was feeling so teary his voice trembled a bit when he talked.

All the men burst into laughter when he said that, and his legs felt so weak that he just wanted to lower himself to the ground and sit there.

"P . . . please can you call him out for me?" A teardrop dribbled from the corner of one of his eyes and slowly made its way down his cheek.

"How stupid can you be, young man? And your father was always ahead of me in class!" The giggly man said before bursting into laughter once more.

"Come on, don't laugh at the child," the friendlier man with the long grey-streaked beard admonished, but Ahmed could see clearly that even he was trying hard not to burst out laughing.

"Son, there is no kind way to tell you this; when you handed over that money to Zuberi, that was the last time you would ever see it. There is a corridor inside this *duka, and* he walked out through the back door." Ahmed suddenly felt an urge to go the bathroom. He slowly sat down on the ground. What on earth was he going to tell Ma Rahma? And the money was not even hers. Where was she going to get so much money for the other women to pay for their wedding sarees? He could feel his head turning. Suddenly, he wasn't strong enough to even sit up. He slowly lay down and curled up in the dust.

C H A P T E R 3

LEAVING TOWN

Fan him more gently," someone was saying when Ahmed came back to his senses. "Sprinkle some more water on his face . . . like this . . ." another voice said and Ahmed felt a chilly splash on this face. He sat up quickly and shook his head violently.

"Oh! *Alhamdulillah,* you are back to life!" the man who was always giggling said sarcastically, lifting his hands to the sky.

"Don't make fun of the child, Abdul. Don't you see he is in trouble?" the bearded man, Kureishi, said harshly.

"Go and explain this to Ma Rahma. She will surely understand you."

"No!" Ahmed shouted louder than he intended, as he fully recalled what had happened.

There was no way he could go back home without the money. His dad was going to be really mad! And he couldn't even begin to imagine what his mother was going to say. It was just unimaginable. His father was so religious, Ahmed had heard him discuss with his friends about how evil gambling was—up there with murder and stealing from orphans.

Then it occurred to him. It was all Samir's fault! He was sure that Samir had it all planned with Zuberi. But how on earth had he been stupid enough to believe them? He remembered the glances that Zuberi had exchanged with Samir. He started feeling so angry just thinking about it. He was going to skin Samir alive if they ever met! But the problem was that Ma Rahma was going to skin *him* alive if he ever went home without the money or the sarees she had sent him to collect.

"Zuberi must be at the base. If you want to talk to him about your money," Abdul, who Ahmed started thinking was enjoying the incident very much, pointed out.

"Where?" Ahmed asked. He just didn't like the way Abdul was smiling, with all those big, brown stained teeth.

"The base," The long-bearded man, Kureishi, explained, putting his hand gently onto Ahmed's shoulder. "That is where they go to buy all those things they inject into their veins. It's no place for you." If that was where Zuberi was, then it was the place for him to go and get the money back, Ahmed thought grimly. It didn't matter whether or not it was a good or nice place. What on earth were the things they injected into the veins that the man was talking about? Was Zuberi sick?

"Is it . . . a hospital?" he cautiously asked.

Abdul doubled over with laughter. Even the other men laughed a little at that. Usman looked unbelievingly into Ahmed's eyes.

"Exactly how old are you, son? Haven't you ever heard about dope? Drugs?" Ahmed felt like a real idiot. He had heard of people taking narcotics, but it was just one of those things that people talked about and you heard about, like ghosts and genies—things that seemed to be from a totally different world that he was not part of.

"Answer his question first, Usman. The place is a hospital. They always talk about going to cure themselves over there," Abdul said in between giggles.

"Are you sure that you, too, don't go there to cure yourself?" Usman asked, obviously annoyed at Abdul's childish laughter.

"There is no need for you to go to the base, son. It is a dangerous place," Usman warned him again.

But his mind was set. If he was going to get killed at the base then so be it. It would only save him from getting killed at home by one or both of his parents anyway. Usman finally pointed out the general direction of the base. Down the street, then turn into an alley after the big coconut tree near old Zuleika's hut, and then turn right after the big house with the red windows. Ahmed walked briskly down the street, angrily dashing tears from his eyes with his fists.

Every time he thought of Samir, and how he had stupidly listened to the crafty boy's nonsense, he just wished he could go, get hold of Samir, and crush him to a pulp. Every thought of going back home or of either of his parents made him feel like rolling around on the ground and screaming with fear.

All around the street, women were bringing out their evening trays of *mandazi, mahamri,* and *bhajia* for sale. Biti Rahma must have started worrying a lot about him, Ahmed thought. He always helped with her evening *mahamri*. And his father would be asking where he was, because he always accompanied him to the mosque for the evening prayers. They must have started looking for him all over the place. Would his mother admit that she had sent him to the tailor for the women's dresses? And the scariest thing was that the women would be coming to pick up their dresses from Ma Rahma! What was she going to tell them? He just had to find Zuberi. A couple of fishermen were coming up from the beach, with rolled nets over their shoulders. The joyful sounds of playing children filled the air, and the women called to each other from their verandahs, exchanging stories and borrowing cooking utensils from each other.

At the end of the street, almost at the beachfront, Ahmed saw the lane that Usman had described. Ahmed couldn't see beyond a big boulder around which the lane seemed to go. He walked briskly past the boulder for some distance before he started hearing voices. He stopped for a while. The voices sounded drunk. It was as if a lot of drunken people were arguing loudly. The loudest of them sounded like a woman or a man with a very high voice.

Ahmed soon came to an open space, in which there was a hut that was made entirely from palm fronds. There was a man lying on the ground and not moving at all as if he was dead. Some other people, including a woman in a long black *buibui,* were arguing loudly outside the hut. Ahmed slowly moved towards the hut. None of the people seemed to have heard him.

"I need my share. He owed me a lot of money, in fact," one of the men was saying loudly, gesturing with his hands as he spoke.

"It doesn't matter. You were not around when the goods were here. He who is not present loses his share," one of the others stammered in a drunken voice. Ahmed could clearly see the drool at the corners of his mouth.

"Who is that kid?" someone else asked angrily, noticing Ahmed at last. "We don't want any strangers—police informers! Who have you come with?" The rest of them stared at him. He was so afraid that he stopped in his tracks.

"Is that your son, Zuhura?" the man who had noticed him first asked with annoyance, as if it was such a horrible thing for one to have a son.

"No!" the woman said heatedly after glancing at Ahmed. Above his fear, Ahmed couldn't help being amazed that the woman had behaved as if she was far too good to be his mother! She had nothing on Ma Rahma, who was always very proud to show him around to whoever she could!

"I'm . . . err . . . looking for Zuberi," he said in a low voice that they all heard.

"Oh, there he is!" One of the men pointed at the one lying quietly on the ground towards the other side of the hut. Ahmed quickly walked over and looked closer. It indeed was Zuberi!

Ahmed bent over the man. At least he was not dead. Was the money still in his pockets? He swiftly tried to pull away the soiled kanzu and check Zuberi's trouser pockets.

"What on earth are you looking for?" the woman asked as the rest of them stared at Ahmed.

"My . . . my money," Ahmed whimpered tearfully as he frantically tried to turn Zuberi over.

"*Ya Rabbi!*" the woman exclaimed. "This man owes the whole world money—even kids!"

"Did he owe you money?" one of the men asked. "You definitely will not find any in his pockets now, but had you come an hour ago, he was as rich as an Arab sheikh! But now it's all gone." Ahmed gasped with shock and stared at the man who had just spoken. "My mother will kill me!" he gasped, tears streaming down his cheeks. They just stared back at him in shock, not understanding him at all.

"Did he steal from you?" one of them asked at last.

"He said he was going to use the money to bet for me! He was going to make millions . . ." Ahmed stopped talking when he realized how stupid he must sound to the strangers.

"Goodness!" The woman covered her mouth in shock. "The rascal! He would stoop right down to the ground to get money for his dope!"

"He conned you. You will never see that money again," one of the men said in a gentle voice, the words and the voice both reminding Ahmed of Usman. He had said almost exactly the same thing in just about the same way. The tears were flowing freely down Ahmed's face now.

"This is a place where people buy drugs. People like Zuberi," the tall man explained.

"Say people like *you*! Why are you taking yourself out of it?" the other one said with a loud guffaw.

"Was I talking to you . . . you . . . baboon!" The tall one shook his fist at him.

"I will mix you up so nicely your mother in Bombolulu will not recognize you, idiot!" He started moving towards the other man.

"*Aka!* Are you going to fight in front of the child?" The woman asked as if she was profoundly shocked. Ahmed felt too weak to rise up from the ground. What was he ever going to do?

"How much money did you say he stole from you?" she asked.

Ahmed was about to explain that Zuberi had not stolen from him. He was just going to use the money to bet for him so that they could make much more money. But then he thought better of it. Somehow the more he talked about that, the more it seemed like the stupidest idea ever, and the more he wondered how on earth he had allowed himself to be convinced to hand over the money.

"Six thousand shillings," he said in a weak voice.

The way Zuhura's eyes popped out as she covered her open mouth with one hand made Ahmed even more worried than he had been. Was six thousand shillings such a shockingly large amount of money?

"Are your parents very rich people?" the woman asked him.

Biti Rahma sold *ukwaju*, spices, mahamri, *bhajia*, and other snacks just like most of the women who lived along their street in Kigogoni, and Ahmed's father had a small retail shop. Ahmed was not very sure exactly what rich meant, but he didn't quite think that his parents were rich.

"No," he said uncertainly.

"*Haya*! The milk has already spilled. You cannot put it back into the bottle." The woman shrugged her thin shoulders. "I'm sure your parents will understand if you just explain it to them. Ahmed felt the tears prick the back of his eyelids again. The problem was that there was absolutely no way that he could think of going home without the clothes that he had been sent to pick up or the money that he had been given.

"No, I can't go back home." He put his head in his hands.

"*Ya Rabbi!* Now what are you going to do?" the woman seemed to be thinking deeply. The men had already moved away and continued their argument. Zuberi had turned over and was snoring louder with no idea of what was going on around him. No one cared about his problems. Life just went on! Even Zuberi was not in any condition to care. He probably had done to other people what he had just done to Ahmed. He did not care.

"God doesn't throw away his own. Come with me. It is getting late," Zuhura said after thinking for a while. Following the lady didn't seem like a very good idea to Ahmed, but then he didn't have very many options. He slowly stood up and took one last look at Zuberi before following Zuhura. The parents of the few friends he had knew his parents. He could not squat at their homes without their parents immediately informing his parents.

CHAPTER 4

A BRIGHT IDEA!

"Mama! Salima pinched my ear!" a little girl's piping voice rang out as soon as Zuhura and Ahmed entered the small mud-walled house. Ahmed had tried to memorize the way they had come but had become confused after the first few turns. They had turned into so many alleys and paths before they arrived at Zuhura's house. All the way, Zuhura had been talking non-stop, but Ahmed's mind had been so full of so many thoughts that he had not heard much of what she was saying.

"She's lying!" an older girl shouted from the other room of the house, which seemed a little bit smaller than his parent's house. The other girl then came rushing from the back room, talking in a complaining voice, but she stopped when she realized that her mother had brought a visitor home.

"You children are going to kill me with stress! *Aka!*" Zuhura said. Ahmed thought she had spoken too loudly. The girls would have heard her quite well had she just talked in a normal voice.

"Have you taken your bath?" Zuhura asked the younger girl who had clasped her around the knees and was now staring at Ahmed with one of her fingers stuck firmly into her mouth.

"I tried to bathe her, but she has refused," the older girl said sulkily, swiveling her head as she talked, which amused Ahmed so much. That was exactly what his sister Suya sometimes did. He must have smiled unintentionally, because Salma blushed and quickly went back into the other room.

"What are you running away from, a big grown woman like you!" Zuhura shouted after the girl. She was getting louder by the minute. And she hadn't offered Ahmed a place to sit, so he just sat on the wobbly old sofa that was along one wall.

"These children will kill me!" Zuhura spread out her hands towards Ahmed. For a brief horrified moment, Ahmed thought she had forgotten that he was just a kid too. It looked as if she thought he was a fellow grown-up whom she could complain to about her children. That was until she said, "To a rich child like you, this place must be so dirty, but it is all we have. Since you won't go back to your parents, then you have to share it with us. Until Allah gives you some other way."

She kicked off her sneakers and kind of collapsed on the floor; she just suddenly sat down with a thud and made some hissy groaning noises with her face all crunched up. For a moment, Ahmed thought she had broken something when she sat down. To his relief, though, she stopped making the groaning sounds, stretched out her feet and reached out her arms to the little girl, who was still looking quietly at Ahmed with such sweet, innocent but teary eyes and one of her fingers still inside her mouth.

To Ahmed's surprise, the little girl walked over to Zuhura, who opened her *buibui and* unbuttoned her blouse as the child sat in her lap and proceeded to suckle. She must have been at least four, Ahmed thought—a bit too old to still be suckling. He shifted uneasily on the seat. Zuhura had gone very quiet at last. She started to slowly nod as Ahmed watched with fascination. The house was deadly quiet, except for the sounds the little girl made as she suckled, and the soft, buzzing snoring that soon started coming from Zuhura's mouth as her head slowly moved and rested on one of her shoulders.

Ahmed started wondering if he could go out where it was definitely cooler. Zuhura did not seem to have air-conditioning in her house as in his parent's house, which had a large bedroom for his parents and a smaller one where his two sisters slept. He had an outer room next to the outdoor kitchen. His room was about as large as the one he was now sitting in. The radio was always on, except in the evenings when their father turned on the television to watch the evening news. He and his sisters were not allowed to watch much television, because his dad always said that they should be outdoors being active most of the time when they were through with their chores and schoolwork.

He suddenly heard a quiet, scrambling noise, and noticed to his amusement that the older girl was peeping at him from around the door to the other room. Why was she so shy? She was a bit bigger than Suya although younger than him—definitely too old to be so shy and afraid of visitors that were just kids like herself. He wanted to smile and talk to her, to ask if there was some work he could help with, but as soon as she noticed that he was looking at her, she immediately ducked back into the other room. Ahmed stood up and went outside to see if he could figure out exactly where he was and to just catch the cool evening breeze.

The place looked pretty much like his neighborhood. The coral and mud-walled houses huddled together were mostly thatched with coconut fronds and looked very much like the ones on his street. The tall coconut trees swaying in the cool evening breeze were like the ones that grew all around his home and everywhere else in Kilifi town for that matter. Was he still in Kigogoni? He had been too worried to ask Zuhura. They had walked for quite some distance from the curing place.

There was an old bench leaning against the wall of Zuhura's house. He gingerly sat down on it, put his chin in his hands and started to sadly think of his home. Ma Rahma would be beside herself with anger and worry, and his father would be furious! He was sure he was going to catch quite some trouble if and when he went back. No, there was no way that he could ever go back home. Perhaps if he could find a job, he could make some money, and then Ma Rahma would not be so angry if he gave it all back. The problem was that he did not know how long it took to make six thousand shillings or the kind of job that he could do to earn that kind of money. Just thinking about it made him much more worried.

He bent over and wiped his face with the edge of his shirt, and when he looked up, there was a man staring down at him! He was so startled that he fell off the bench. The man did not even apologize. He just kept looking down at him with an angry look on his face. Ahmed had heard of *djinnis*, spirits of the sea that appeared and disappeared. He had thought they were just stories. Now he was convinced that he could be seeing a *djinni*!

"What are you doing here?" he finally asked in a low tone.

"I . . . I came with Zuhura," Ahmed stammered. The man looked like he was going to kick him or beat him up. He was so tall and thin, with a rough beard all around his narrow face. His eyes were bloodshot and he didn't seem to ever blink.

"Yes? You came with Zuhura from where?" the man asked. Ahmed thought of darting off from the bench and running away, but he was so tired and hungry. To his dismay, teardrops oozed out of his eyes and made their way down each check. He dashed them away with his fists.

"Why are you crying? Have I asked you to cry or to tell me where you came from with Zuhura?" the man asked, spreading his hands with wonder.

"Zuhura, *eee*!" he suddenly shouted towards the door of the house.

"What is it, Sudi? You have woken the baby!" Zuhura answered loudly from the house. The man must have woken her too, because she also sounded a little sleepy.

"Who is this? Where did you find him?" Sudi asked in his gruff voice.

"I found him in town. He lost some money his parents told him to take somewhere. Now he is afraid to go back home," Zuhura explained as she came out of the house.

"How did he lose it?" Sudi asked suspiciously. "Do you and those friends of yours have anything to do with it?"

"Me and what friends of mine? Can you even listen to yourself talk?" Zuhura retorted.

"How did you lose your money, young man?" Sudi turned his attention to Ahmed without answering Zuhura.

"Zuberi took it to bet with." Ahmed explained.

"Isn't Zuberi one of your drug-taking friends?" Sudi turned again to Zuhura.

"And what if he is? Would it be better if he was my enemy?" Zuhura answered. At that point, the little girl started crying from inside the house. Zuhura clicked her tongue and went back inside, picking the little girl up as she went. Sudi took the basket he had been carrying into the house. Ahmed noticed that it had some fish and some paper-wrapped packages.

"Please cook an early supper. I have a job tonight," said Sudi.

"I hope this one has more money than the one you did the other day," Zuhura answered in a lower voice than the one with which she had spoken earlier.

"I think the boy will be useful in . . . you know." Ahmed overheard the man mumble. He was growing more pleasant by the minute. Perhaps it was because he had assured himself that Ahmed was just a harmless kid.

"No, you don't know what he is like or who he even is." Zuhura definitely thought she was talking in a whisper that Ahmed couldn't hear, but he heard her coarse, grating voice quite well.

"He is an innocent . . . and desperate. If we tell him what to do, he will do it. Didn't you say he has run away from home?" Sudi asked. It was so strange that they were already discussing him in low, pleasant tones. Then there was some job that Sudi was going to ask him to help with, and just a few minutes earlier they had seemed to be quarrelling quite heatedly!

Suddenly, Ahmed felt more cheerful though. If this man had a job for him, he was going to do it very willingly! He hoped he was going to be paid six thousand shillings so that he could go back home. He was so eager that he wanted to go back into the house and tell Sudi that he was ready to do the job whatever it was. But then, just in time, it occurred to him that they would realize that he had been listening to everything they had been saying. Sudi came out, looking even friendlier.

"So, what did you say your name was?" he asked in a gentle tone. Ahmed was sure he hadn't told him his name before, but it didn't seem nice to point that out.

"I need you to help with a job tonight, but you have to be very brave," he continued in the same gentle tone as he sat down beside Ahmed and put his hand on the boy's shoulder. Ahmed nodded silently.

"Will you help me with the job?" Sudi asked again. Ahmed wanted to ask how much Sudi was going to pay him, but he decided that it was not very polite to do so. What was important was that he had a job now! God was definitely watching over him up there somewhere.

CHAPTER 5

THE JOB

The evening breeze was gently blowing in from the sea, and it was getting comfortingly cooler. The sun had set, and a few stars were already blinking in the sky here and there. Zuhura had spread some mats outside, and Sudi was sitting on them, alongside Ahmed and three men who had joined them. Zuhura had served them rice and fish on two platters. They all ate with their hands, sharing the food between them. Ahmed sat towards the very end of one of the mats. The mats reminded him so much of the prayer mats that he and his father used when they prayed. He couldn't remember ever missing the evening prayers, ever since he was just a baby.

"So, this small master will go in there for us?" one of the men, whom Ahmed had heard the others call Bakri, asked.

"Een-he!" Sudi nodded his head gently. In the couple of hours that Ahmed had been at his house, he had decided that he really liked Sudi. After their first meeting, he had turned out to be very friendly.

He had instructed Salima, his older daughter, to take out some bathing water for Ahmed in the palm frond bathroom behind the house. Then he had sent her to the shop for some dates and orange juice, which Ahmed had really enjoyed as they waited for supper to be ready. He had been so hungry. Sudi had then talked gently to him, asking him about his home, his parents and a lot of other things. The more answers he gave, the more Sudi seemed to like him. He still didn't know what type of job he was being employed to do, but he was very sure that Sudi was going to pay him six thousand shillings. He was going to work very hard at whatever the job was, and Sudi was going to be very impressed. Who knew? Perhaps even after he went home, he could still come back and do more jobs for Sudi. Then he would use the money he earned to bet on Sportbet and win those millions after all. But, of course, he would find someone more reliable than Zuberi to bet for him. He felt a twinge of anger as he thought about Zuberi and that rascal Samir. God help him whenever they met again! Ahmed's plans for the future were interrupted by Bakri touching his shoulder.

"Do you need something to give you more courage for the job?" he asked.

"He doesn't know all that," Sudi answered before Ahmed could figure out what the man was talking about.

"Actually, he has never done such a job." Sudi disclosed what he had apparently not told the others yet.

"*What!*" the other men exclaimed unbelievingly.

"But I'm going to work very hard!" Ahmed said quickly before he could stop himself. He was so afraid of losing whatever job it was. All the men laughed, lightening up the mood.

"This job doesn't need you to work hard . . . it needs you to work smart, like a rabbit," the man who had asked first explained, gently patting him on the shoulder. Ahmed thought that things were getting even nicer! He wasn't going to get all sweaty and tired doing the job after all!

"Explain it to him, Sudi," Selemani said.

"We need you to get inside a house for us," Sudi explained, lowering his voice even more, after furtively glancing around. For a moment, Ahmed just stared at him. Were they going to employ him as some kind of watchman?

"There are some things we want to get out of the house. You will go there, tell the owners of the house that you are lost and that you need somewhere to spend the night. When everyone else has gone to sleep, you will open the door and get for us . . ." Sudi explained further. Ahmed slowly started realizing that the men wanted him to help them to rob a house. They were thieves!! He lost his appetite. He couldn't even swallow the food in his mouth.

"Hey, we are not bad people. The people in that house have something that belongs to us. They won't give it back, so we just want to take it, nothing more!"

"Yes!" Selemani agreed, "If we were bad people, we would break into the house and kill the people and then rob them. That is what bad people do. All we want is to peacefully collect our property and then go away."

Ahmed had been so easily tricked just a few hours ago, and he really doubted that what he was being told was true. But then, he was so desperate. He really needed the job. He needed the six thousand shillings to give back to Ma Rahma. He would still get a beating for sure, but at least the women would have their money back for the wedding sarees. He didn't have a lot of options just then.

"Even if we were stealing, you would not be the one doing so. You will just be opening the door, and even God can't punish you for that," Sudi reassured him. The food in Ahmed's mouth became easy to swallow again. But he had completely lost his appetite. It was a really scary job, even if it sounded so easy. If his father ever found out about it, he would never forgive him. In just a few hours, it seemed like he had done all manners of things that he had been raised to believe were absolutely evil! But if he was going to ever go back home to his parents, he had to do the job. In his mind, they would not even accept him back without the money. He had to make it, one way or another.

"Okay, I will do it." He firmly nodded his head. The men all thumped him on the back and told him what a brave and smart boy he was. He decided to ask about the payment, while they still thought so highly of him and liked him so dearly.

"Uhhmm . . . how much will you pay me? Six thousand shillings?" he asked slowly, as politely as he could. The men looked at him with surprise for a moment, Selemani and Bakri's eyes slightly popping out.

"What th—" Bakri started speaking, but Selemani quickly slapped him hard on one leg.

"A mosquito!" Selemani exclaimed as Bakri squealed with pain. There were many mosquitoes buzzing around, but Ahmed was smart enough to realize that the slap was to stop Bakri from saying what he had been about to say, not protect him from the insects.

"But, of course, we are going to pay you six thousand shillings, my good boy!" Selemani quickly assured Ahmed.

"Yes!" Sudi nodded his head eagerly, "Everything for you, my son." Ahmed thought of his father again when Sudi called him that. His father would never make him do such a job. But if he was going to return home with the money he had lost, then he had to go ahead and do the job for the men.

After the meal was over and the dishes had been cleared away by Zuhura, Sudi went into the house and brought back a large paper bag, from which he removed black sweaters and woolen caps. After the men had put them on, even Ahmed found it hard to see them unless they moved. He was allowed to be in his white kanzu though, but Sudi handed him a light jumper with buttons. It was obviously a girl's, most certainly Salma's. Ahmed didn't like putting on a girl's jumper, but the night was becoming chillier by the minute, and besides, he didn't want to make a lot of fuss. He just wanted the six thousand shillings as soon as possible so that he could go back home. Soon, they were walking briskly down one of the several narrow alleys in the town, with the men talking in low tones.

"We have to get the boy inside the house early. They usually go to bed by ten," Ahmed heard Selemani whispering. In between the men's conversation, the only sounds that could be heard were those of their feet squelching in the sandy soil along the paths and alleys. Whenever they passed houses, they could hear the voices of people as they chatted and had their evening meal. Soon they came to a place where there seemed to be bigger houses, each of which with a wall made of coral stones around it, and a wide, locked iron gate. They slowly walked past three of the houses before stopping in front of one.

"Here we are . . ." Ahmed could see Selemani's teeth glittering in the dim light as the man patted his shoulder and smiled down at him. "Remember what we instructed you to say—that you were on a bus going to Lamu with your mother, and you got off to buy some medicine for her when the bus stopped in town." Sudi had slowly coached Ahmed earlier with the story he was to tell the house's owners, but for some reason Selemani found it necessary to repeat it. Ahmed was supposed to then tearfully explain that the shopkeeper had delayed his change and that the impatient bus driver had driven off without him. Ahmed felt so hot and his heart was pounding so fast that he could clearly hear it.

"There is a knob that operates this gate on the verandah wall."

Selemani refreshed Ahmed's memory. They had already told him that, and about the small shelf in one corner of the living room where the door keys were kept. Bakri had worked as a house servant for the people that lived in that house and he knew where everything was kept. He also knew the people well enough to be sure that they will tell Ahmed to sleep on a couch in the living room. Sudi then rang the gate bell before the three men scampered into the shadows, their dark clothes rendering them totally invisible. A tall young man opened the gate after a while. Ahmed was so scared by that time that he stammered when he tried to explain.

"Yes, what is it?" The young man asked anxiously, looking down at Ahmed with a concerned frown on his face.

"The bus . . . left me . . . my mother . . . Lamu . . ." Ahmed mumbled nervously, his whole body shaking from fear, and only a few jumbled-up words of the story he had been coached to tell came out. The young man gently stepped back and told him to get inside the compound before closing the gate behind them.

"Who is it, Swabri?" a woman's voice called from inside the house.

"It is just a kid . . . the bus left him . . . or something," the young man answered sympathetically. As they entered the house, a heavily built old lady stood up from the couch on which she had been sitting and waddled over to Ahmed.

"*Maskiiini!*" she exclaimed, "Oh, you poor child! How could the bus driver be so heartless! People are so evil nowadays."

For a moment, Ahmed felt so bad that he was tricking these nice people. Then he thought again about the six thousand shillings that he was going to be paid by Sudi and his friends after the job. Then he was going to be able to go back home, and everything would be fine. Perhaps he could just go to the mosque afterwards and ask God to forgive him. There did not seem to be a lot of other ways at the moment.

A short, thin, old man with a long, white beard and glasses with shiny round lenses came in from one of the inner rooms and peered shortsightedly at Ahmed as the old lady explained what the problem was.

"Give him some food, Swabri. Visitors come from God," the old man finally said as he toddled over to the couch with the help of a stout walking stick. This made Ahmed feel guilty again. He was sure that he wasn't exactly a visitor that had come from God. He forced himself to eat some of the noodles and minced meat that Swabri gave him, sitting at a table in the adjacent dining room. Two young women, a boy and a girl almost his age and two men, older than Swabri, soon came to watch TV with the old folks in the living room, the grown-ups all expressing their sympathy with Ahmed and their anger at the imaginary driver for leaving the boy behind.

Before long, though, they forgot all about Ahmed as they got engrossed in the news, heatedly discussing among themselves the things the politicians in the news had done and said. Ahmed felt calmer by then. He felt like he could carry out the job quite easily. He looked around slowly and soon located the small shelf on which the house keys were kept. He had not noticed the small knob in the verandah when he came because he had been so nervous, but he was very sure he was going to find it exactly as Selemani had described it. He slowly removed Salma's jumper and folded it gently in his lap. He was feeling so tired and sleepy. He had walked longer that day than he could remember ever walking before. An overwhelming tiredness overcame him until he couldn't keep his eyes open any longer.

"*Maskiiini.* he is getting sleepy," the old lady observed, interrupting the excited discussion the others were having.

"Swabri, get him a nice mat."

"Where will he be sleeping?" one of the younger ladies whom Ahmed had heard being called Amina asked.

"Here in the living room over in that corner, of course," Swabri answered.

"Why not in your room?" Amina insisted. Swabri gave her a glare that made her look aside.

"Okay! Don't fight over where he should sleep. I'm sure he will be just fine sleeping over in that corner, on the nice comfortable mat that Swabri is going to fetch him right now." The old lady looked pointedly at Swabri, who took the clue and went down the corridor, coming back after a few minutes with a mat, which he set up in a corner of the spacious sitting room. The other two men excused themselves and retired to other parts of the large house, and the two children went away quietly after a few more minutes. In the dry, humid climate, one did not need blankets—perhaps just the slightest of sheets to cover up in bed—but they did need mosquito nets. There were quite a few mosquitoes already buzzing around irritatingly.

"Over there in that corner," the old lady directed. "Make sure you don't put it over a stone that will hurt this creature of God." Swabri deftly spread the mat in the corner and patted it down all over to see if there could be the stone that the old lady had warned him about. He kept looking over his shoulder at the television. Ahmed drowsily wondered what it was that he was so nervous about. Then the sports news came on. At precisely that time, one of the younger women took the remote to switch channels.

"Hey! What do you think you are doing?" Swabri shouted, startling her.

"I want to switch to something else. The news is over," the lady answered.

"This boy and football. He wants to watch the sports news!" said the old man who had dozed on and off a number of times.

"Sports is boring," the young lady started saying, but Swabri had walked over and grabbed the remote from her before she could finish saying whatever she was going to say and swiftly switched back to the sports news.

"Your teams won't make it, like yesterday, you will lose everything you used on Sportbet!" the aggrieved lady said, pouting her lips in a way that reminded Ahmed so much of Sabrina and Zuhura's daughter. The other lady giggled with amusement.

"Don't curse your brother Sauda!" the old lady said, pretending to be annoyed, but even Ahmed from his mat in the corner could see that she was also quite amused.

"Swabri *baba*, you will win all those millions, and you will buy your mother some *halua* and a beautiful set of *lesos*, won't you?" Both younger women giggled from behind their hands.

"Haya! You keep on laughing, I will win *inshallah*, and we will see who will be laughing then!" The mention of Sportbet had driven all the sleep away from Ahmed's eyes. Swabri also did Sportbet? Then he remembered Sudi and his gang waiting outside for him to unlock the door, and he had that cold feeling in the pit of his stomach. He curled up on the mat, but all the sleep had gone out of his eyes. What if he came up with another plan? Did he have to be part of what Sudi was planning? Now that he could think clearly, he could think differently. Sudi and his pals' intention may not be simply a matter of taking something that belonged to them without harming that wonderful family as they had said. Ahmed already liked Swabri, and the old lady had been so nice to him, just the way his mother would have been. What if Sudi and his men wanted to harm those wonderful people? He found it strange that grown people couldn't just go to the house, knock on the door, and ask for something if indeed it belonged to them. Something was definitely wrong. He slowly turned over and curled up on the other side. He always seemed to think better from the right side. He breathed slowly, pretending to be asleep as he thought deeper and listened to Swabri and the women argue. The old lady had helped the old man to bed after he almost hit his head on the table, dozing.

"I bet two hundred shillings only. What would that buy anyway?" Swabri was asking his sister, Sauda. The other lady was the wife of Swabri's brother because he had heard both Swabri and Sauda call her *wifi*, but the older lady kept calling her 'Anisa, my child.' The old man was Mansur, and he kept calling the old lady Bi Maimuna although all the others addressed her as Mama.

"It could buy you a new vest. That one is so torn up!" Sauda giggled.

"And how is it any of your business? I can go out and make more than two hundred in a day!" Swabri argued gruffly.

"Oh, leave him alone, will you? Will you laugh too when he wins those millions?" Anisa swiped her palm at Sauda.

"Are these the type of people that win millions?" Sauda's tinkling laughter bounced across the room.

"You will wake up the boy. What is all this noise about!" Swabri admonished angrily.

"Oh, I'm so sorry," Sauda said, not really sounding sorry.

Ahmed decided he liked her. She was sassy and a tease just like Sabrina. He smiled to himself, listening to them joking and teasing each other. He did not want anything bad to happen to them. But what were Sudi and his men going to do to him if he failed them? Well, he was going to find out what was going to happen, when it happened. He started growing drowsier until he slipped off into deep sleep.

A NEW DAY

Allahu Akbar!" the soft murmur startled Ahmed. For a moment, he couldn't remember where he was. He wildly wondered what he was doing on a mat on the floor and quickly sat up. The light was on in the room, and Mansur was saying his morning prayers. Ahmed knew enough not to disturb the old man as he said his prayers but he wondered whether he should join him. He always joined his father every morning. He decided to just sit up and watch. It didn't seem very polite to remain lying down while Mansur said his prayers. Then it didn't seem quite right to just sit there and watch, so he got up. And before he knew it, he just found himself praying, saying the familiar words after Mansur. After the final *Allahu Akbar*, Mansur wiped his face and smiled warmly at Ahmed.

"Shikamoo." Ahmed bowed down respectfully. His mother had always told him that he should always greet elders first.

"Marahabaa!" Mansur replied cheerfully. "You are up already!" "Yes, sir," Ahmed replied not knowing what else to say. After all, he was up already!

"Those lazy ones are still snoring and dreaming in their sleep," Mansur bent down slightly and said in a whisper as if he was divulging a very deep secret. Ahmed smiled conspiringly, like someone who had been let in on a close secret.

"Let me switch on the television for you!" the old man said in the same excited whisper, as if turning on the TV was such a fun and mysterious thing they had to do before everyone else woke up and caught them at it.

He toddled over with some difficulty, because he did not have his stout walking stick and peered at the bottom of the screen for a while. Then he remembered that he had not switched on the power, clucking his tongue and doing so. Ahmed wondered why he didn't use the remote. Perhaps he did not know how to operate the TV after all.

"The remote . . ." he said after clearing his throat nervously. "Uhh . . . what?" Mansur looked startled.

"Use the remote. It's easier." Ahmed pointed to the remote that was on the table.

"Oooh, use it then," Mansur said and chortled with amusement, as if Ahmed had said a very funny thing. "I don't have my glasses."

Somehow Ahmed felt that even if he had glasses, Mansur would still not be able to use the remote. He walked over and switched the TV on as Mansur eagerly went over to the settee and sat down. The Sportbet ad was on. It seemed to Ahmed that Sportbet was out to haunt him.

Immediately, he remembered what had brought him to the house and how he had let down Sudi and his men. He started getting very worried. He had been so desperate to earn the money to give back to his mother that he had not allowed himself to think harder about what the men seemed like. But right there in Mansur's living room away from them, he concluded that they were not the men that he would like to cross at all.

He stared at the screen. There was a grinning man that had won twenty million shillings saying how easy it had been. Ahmed felt eager to try and bet once more. Before the incident with Samir and Zuberi, he had not had the slightest interest in betting. But since hearing that someone had bet just two hundred shillings and won a truckload of money, his mind, in between worrying about a thousand and one things, kept wandering back to exactly what he could do with such a lot of money. Then a bulb lit up somewhere in his mind. He was going to ask Mansur for a job so as to earn some money to bet with. Then he would win big and be able to give his mother the six thousand shillings meant for the women's sarees, and still have a lot more to do with as he wished. He looked at Mansur from the corner of his eye. The old man didn't seem to be quite with it. Plus, the old lady, Bi Maimuna, seemed to be the one in charge. Everyone else seemed to obey everything she said. He was going to have to come up with an excuse to stick around long enough to earn some money to bet with. He toyed with the idea of just confessing and getting it over and done with, but he quickly dismissed it. It would mean having to confess that he was going to help a gang of thugs to break into the house the previous day. Okay, not exactly a gang—just three—but still . . .

"Do you like the cartoon things?" Mansur asked, still with the cheeky smile and low whisper. He seemed to really be enjoying Ahmed's company. But Ahmed was too worried about how things were going to turn out to enjoy anything. Not even the hot spicy tea that Sauda and her sister-in-law served later that morning. He was dreading the moment when they would ask him if he shouldn't be going on his way. He was sure they expected him to be anxious about catching up with his mother in Lamu or going back home, to assure his people that he was alright. But no one seemed to remember all that. They just woke up and went about their business. The two older men had their breakfast and left, and the two children were driven somewhere in the big black Pajero soon after breakfast.

The first thing that Swabri did when he woke up was to go for a copy of the day's newspaper from a vendor just a few meters away from the gate. He absorbed himself in it, pausing from time to time to take long sips from his cup. He took his phone from his pocket and a much folded and unfolded piece of paper from another pocket. Then he started closely studying the newspaper's sports page, comparing something from it to what was written on the piece of paper before carefully typing on the phone. He did this with so much concentration that he didn't notice Ahmed staring at him intently, even when he moved closer to him on the settee.

"Are you betting?" Ahmed asked quietly, but Swabri was so startled by the unexpected sound of his voice that he burst out laughing and Ahmed joined him.

"You shouldn't be sneaking up on people like that. Do you want me to die of a heart attack?" he asked cheerfully.

"I'm sorry," Ahmed answered timidly.

"No, it's okay, have you had your breakfast?" Swabri asked cheerfully, but Ahmed could see that his attention was distracted again. He had already started going through a column on the piece of paper, using his pen up and down, the serious frown forming on his face once more.

"Do you sometimes win a lot of money?" Ahmed asked in a low voice.

"Huh?" Swabri grunted absent mindedly, "Oh! Yeah! I win some from time to time."

"Can you help me win too?" Ahmed pressed on. Swabri slowly put aside his book and looked at Ahmed with a new interest.

"How old are you again?" Ahmed was slightly built and looked smaller and younger than a lot of children his age, and he was used to people thinking he was younger than he really was.

"Fourteen," he said slowly, quite sure that Swabri wasn't going to believe him.

"Are you sure?" Swabri definitely doubted.

"Yes, I am. It's only that I look smaller than that; it's just my size," Ahmed assured him.

"Oh. Alright then," Swabri shrugged his shoulders, "but you know you have to be at least eighteen to be allowed to bet, don't you? And also, you need money," he added in a matter of fact manner.

"If I find some money, will you help me to bet?" Ahmed asked anxiously.

"Okay, why not?" Swabri nodded and patted him on the shoulder. It was like he was just being nice because he thought it was so cute, but Ahmed didn't want to be cute. He wanted money—six thousand shillings to give to his mother and more money for all the things he had dreamt of.

"But shouldn't you be going home or something?" Swabri asked, "Won't your mother be worried?"

"No, I don't think so. She knows I will be back." Ahmed attempted to make a brave smile, but the fact was that he was very worried about his mother, Ma Rahma, not the imaginary one that had lost him on the way to Lamu. Also, about Zuhura and Sudi and his gang and just generally about everything that he thought could happen that day. But above all that worry, he wanted to bet and make the money he needed. Then everything else would cease to matter.

"So, what is there that one can do for work around here?" Ahmed asked. Swabri was once more lost in deep thought.

"Huh? What? Ohh . . . I guess you could help Mariam with the kitchen work," he said absently. Ahmed had helped his mother. Perhaps if he helped the house help with the work. they would pay him. Even if it was just two hundred shillings, he thought that was enough to bet with and perhaps win the jackpot, or was it called jackfruit? He wasn't sure. He could wash utensils and even cook some dishes. He felt his mood lighten up.

"Where is the kitchen?" Ahmed asked.

"Oh, around the back of the house," said Swabri. Ahmed immediately stood up and started heading towards where Swabri had pointed. A few steps ahead, he turned around and looked at Swabri. He was engrossed once more in moving the pen slowly up and down the list on the scrap of paper, stopping to enter certain numbers into his phone with the utmost concentration.

Ahmed slowly moved past the wreck of a big lorry that had been laying in the yard for quite a while. The yard itself was bigger and the house much larger than it had seemed last night when he arrived. There was a flock of about fifteen hens pecking around, and a frisky little puppy ran over wagging its tail excitedly and romped around Ahmed's feet. He deftly side-stepped it and continued to the kitchen. He heard someone humming a popular *taraab* tune as he got closer to the kitchen. The voice was a bit shaky, and as Ahmed got closer, he realized that the person singing was an old lady, much older than Bi Maimuna.

"*Shikamoo,*" he greeted politely.

"*Marahaba.*" The old lady peered closely at him, such that she seemed to be quite angry. But it was the wrinkles, so many more than Ahmed had ever seen on anyone's face before. She seemed to not be able to see very well because she squinted and peered at him, first from one eye, and then the other.

"Are you Swalehe's son? Did your mother send you for the money?" she asked, the look on her face turning more anxious than it had been. Ahmed could hear the breath wheezing in and out of her lungs.

"No, I'm Ahmed, Swabri sent me to help you with the work," he replied. She didn't understand him the first time, so he had to repeat it in a louder voice. She was definitely quite relieved.

"Ahaaa! God bless that nice young man. He really feels pity for those that need pity!" she exclaimed. "I was just about to wash the breakfast utensils. Start with those please." Ahmed looked at the pile of dishes in a corner of the kitchen anxiously.

"Oh, you have to fetch the water from the well," she said and handed him the pail she was holding. "Here I was, wondering how my old back was going to bear lifting one more bucketful from that well. Then God sends his very angel to me to help!" Some of the many wrinkles unfolded as she beamed down at Ahmed. It was very well that she thought him an angel, but he was not so sure that whatever angelic powers he had would enable him to lift up that large pail. She took it and went over to the well that she had pointed out.

He only filled it about halfway, but it took all the strength he could ever summon to carry it back to the kitchen. He had to stand for a few minutes and catch his breath before he started with the pile of dishes. The plates, bowls, and cups were easy-peasy, but the greasy pans and at least four large pots made him homesick and the thoughts of home and what his mother would be doing brought tears to his eyes once again. But how was he ever going to go home without the six thousand shillings? Had the women already reported the incident to the police? Perhaps his mother had already been arrested and it was all his fault. The thought of that made him even more tired than he was to begin with.

"Hey, young man, did I give you the broom for the yard? Oh, silly me! How could I ever forget?" The old lady, who Ahmed had figured out was called Mariam because she had this habit of referring to herself by name, roused him from his thoughts.

"Bi Maimuna always wants the yard clean by this time. Oh, Mariam! How could I ever forget to tell you?" she beamed at Ahmed as if she was divulging something delightful. Ahmed would have preferred to rest some more, but he took the broom and swept the large yard. Somehow having to sweep the entire yard made it look even bigger than he had thought it was. He had to sit down and rest a couple of times, but he managed to finish.

"Oh, such a strong young man," Mariam clucked with what Ahmed thought was a cheeky gleam in her eyes. For one horrified moment, Ahmed though she was going to assign him yet another chore. He decided that he had had about enough. If that was the case, he was going to firmly put his foot down, but to his relief, she pulled out a low stool and invited him to sit down.

"Would you like some water to drink?" she asked and went to fetch some before he could answer. He definitely needed a very cold drink. She poured some water from an old plastic jug into a tumbler and handed it to him. It was surprisingly cold.

"I always take a jugful from the big house," Mariam explained, guessing the question on Ahmed's mind. She fished out an old phone from the many folds in her *buibui* and handed it to Ahmed.

"I need you to help me with something," said Mariam. She took some bottle caps from another fold in her *buibui* and handed them to Ahmed.

"Swabri helps me to do this, but now Allah has sent you to be Mariam's helper, well . . ." For a moment Ahmed was at a loss at what she expected him to do.

"*Aka!* Don't you know these things? There is a number on the back of the bottle caps. You have to send them to the number written on the caps. You know how to read, don't you?" she asked, squinting doubtfully at him.

"Yes!" Ahmed replied quickly, taking the bottle caps from her hand. He was actually at the top of his class. Okay, almost—among the top fifteen at least—he wanted to tell her. How on earth would anyone ever suspect him of not being able to read? Then it occurred to him that the old lady was betting too in some way. His interest was aroused once more.

"Do you also bet the other wa . . . on football?" he asked without expecting her to know what he was saying.

"Oh, I won two thousand shillings last month . . . or was it the month before that? Days just fly by nowadays," she said cheerfully. Just when he was going to ask her if she was going to help him bet, she added, "Swabri did it for me, but I didn't tell him I won. He would have wanted me to give him some of the money, an old widow like me." She clucked her mouth once more. Then Ahmed remembered why he was there in the backyard in the first place. Was she really going to pay him or was he expected to be paid by Mansur? The old man didn't seem like he was the one that paid people at all.

"Is it you who will pay me for the work?" he asked nervously. "What work?" Mariam asked as if she totally had no idea what he was talking about.

"Uhh, what I have just done . . ." He swept his hand over the pile of dishes on the sunning rack and across the yard he had just swept.

"Oh, you were supposed to be paid?" Mariam asked with genuine surprise

"Yes! Swabri said so!".

"Oh, Swabri doesn't do the paying around here. You will have to talk to Bi Maimuna." Ahmed felt a twinge of anxiety at that. Maybe he could convince Swabri to talk to Bi Maimuna for that? Or had he been tricked once more by a grown-up?

"How much is he likely to pay me?" Ahmed asked. It occurred to him right then that previously he never had to worry about money. All he had ever had apart from things like lunch money and allowances on school trips was the little that his mother gave him after sending him on a thousand errands. His father never gave him any money because he had everything he could ever have at home.

"What do you need your money for, food or rent?" his father would ask whenever he caught Ahmed asking for any money. But in the few hours that he had been way from home, suddenly money seemed like a very important thing to him. And he had been taught that he had to work to earn money. The longer and harder he worked, the more money he was going to make.

"Is what I have done all the work that I can help with?" he asked Mariam.

"Oh, no. There is much more work here than an old creaky woman like Mariam could ever do alone," she said with the cheeky gleam that Ahmed had started noticing a lot.

"There are the chickens to feed, then lunch, and after that the lunch dishes," she was actually ticking them off on her fingers as she spoke. Ahmed felt tired just listening. He just needed only two hundred shillings to bet with. He was so sure that if he bet just once, he was going to win big time, just the way Saidi had.

"How much do you think they are going to pay me for all this?" he asked hesitantly.

"Bi Maimuna is not a bad person. She will look at you with nice eyes." Mariam said mysteriously. Ahmed didn't know what to make of that. He didn't need anyone looking at him, with nice or not- nice eyes. He just needed some money to bet with. But then he was so used to grown-ups talking in mysterious ways. Perhaps Mariam just meant that Bi Maimuna was going to pay him well. He chose to believe that and walked over to the henhouse with the pail of food that Mariam had given him. He had never seen so many chickens in one place, and they all rushed at him when he entered, such that he panicked and almost overturned the pail, but he didn't want to do anything that would make result in him not being paid in the end. Some started pecking at his toes, and he was sure he had lost his left little toe. He firmly waded through the mass of noisy chickens to the feeding troughs. He emptied some of the grain and feed in one trough, but did not enjoy the relief of a lot of the chickens going over to that trough, before one of them flew onto his shoulder and would have pecked out his eye had he not quickly brushed it away. But he had to drop the bucket to do that, spilling the feed all over the floor.

"Mama!" he cried out before he could stop. Some of the feed had spilt over his toes and the hens were fighting over it, scratching and pecking at his toes and feet so painfully. He quickly picked up the now empty bucket and rushed out of the house. A few meters from it, he remembered that he had not locked the door to the henhouse and rushed back to do so. Then he sat down and examined his poor toes. About three were bleeding, but thankfully, they were still on his feet. As he was making his way back to the house, he heard the unmistakable loud voice of Zuhura. She was the last person he expected at the house. How on earth did she even get the courage to go to the house that her husband was going to rob the previous day?

"He was seen here. People say they saw him coming here!" Zuhura was angrily saying.

Ahmed suddenly felt so mad! Why was she speaking so loudly? He walked swiftly to where Zuhura was talking with Bi Maimuna, Sauda, and Anisa. Mariam was toddling towards them.

"There you are! Ahmed! Why did you run off the bus?" Zuhura asked angrily.

"What bus . . .?" Ahmed stopped short in his tracks. Was Zuhura totally mad?

"*What bus*? Did you ask me what bus? You've made me come all the way back from Lamu, and you are asking what bus?" Zuhura asked angrily. She began rushing over to Ahmed as if she was going to beat him.

"Aka! Don't kill the poor child!" Bi Maimuna screamed with alarm, and Swabri rushed over and caught her arm to stop her.

"Ya Rabbi! My own child, and now you want to beat me up for correcting him!" Zuhura cried out, looking at her arm that was grasped firmly in Swabri's grip as if Swabri had broken it.

"Wait until you get him back home and kill him there if you want to! We don't want blood in our home!" Swabri said angrily.

"Yes!" Bi Maimuna agreed anxiously. "Lady, take your son away from here. You can sort out whatever it is from wherever you've come from!"

"She's not my mother! I don't even know her!" Ahmed shouted, his voice breaking.

"What bad manners have you been training him in since you kidnapped him?" Zuhura asked heatedly, thrusting her head forward in a way that reminded Ahmed so much of a snake he had seen at the animal orphanage some days earlier. His anger gave way to a deep fear. Was Zuhura even human? The others were so shocked that none of them was speaking. Bi Maimuna had her hand clasped to her chest and Mariam's mouth and eyes were both wide open.

Zuhura's headscarf had slipped back and her hair looked so matted and dirty.

"Come! We should be on our way. You have already wasted enough of my time!" Zuhura was almost screaming as she grasped Ahmed's hand and dragged him out of the compound. Ahmed was so shocked that he was totally speechless. Swabri quickly closed the door after them as they left.

"*Enhe!* So, you thought you were the clever one, didn't you?"

Zuhura grinned evilly at Ahmed as soon as they were a few hundred meters away from the gate. Ahmed was still in shock. His heart was drumming wildly. He was so sure it was the end for him.

"Did you tell them about Sudi and the job you spoiled yesterday?" she asked furiously. Ahmed could only shake his head.

"Yes, I knew you were too stupid to rat us out. You just wanted to live in that big house and be with the rich people, didn't you?" she asked. Ahmed didn't think he was required to answer that. He just stood there panting. His legs felt so weak that he couldn't run away, even though he was thinking of doing so. As they moved further down the path, with Zuhura still scolding loudly and firmly holding onto his hand, Sudi suddenly emerged from some bushes and a few minutes later Selemani came out too.

"Aha! Here is the big boss!" Selemani said sarcastically with a wide grin as he rubbed his hands together. He looked like he thought Ahmed was a delicious meal he was about to sink his big teeth into. This made Ahmed very worried.

"So, you thought you could shake us off just like that?" Sudi asked. The look in his eyes seemed so evil that Ahmed wanted to scream and shout for help. He was so sure that whatever they were going to do to him was not going to be very pleasant.

"I'm . . . I'm so sorry," he stammered. "I fell asleep. I didn't mean to."

"What happened to your feet?" Sudi noticed for the first time that Ahmed's feet were bleeding.

"I was feeding the chicken," he quickly explained.

"Ahaa! So, they didn't let you sit around and dine like a king the way we did! They made you work for your food, huh?" Zuhura seemed so delighted by that. Ahmed hung his head.

"Okay, it doesn't look like it was his fault." Sudi said thoughtfully, "It was the fault of his stupidity."

"Did you tell them what you went to their house to do?" Sudi asked him.

"Nooo!" Ahmed said hotly. Perhaps the way he said it seemed to convince Sudi.

"Okay, enough drama—let's go back home," Sudi said.

Home? Ahmed started having the urge to cry once more. He thought of his real home—how his parents, especially

Ma Rahma, would be beside themselves with worry. He wondered whether the men that had been sitting at the shop verandah had told his parents what had happened. Perhaps his parents had already reported to the police that he was lost. The grown-ups were walking briskly and he had to trot to keep up. Perhaps they wanted to get as far away from Mansur's house as possible.

"Did your bet get some money yesterday?" Zuhura asked Sudi. "Why?" Sudi asked gruffly, "You need money to buy your powder?"

"What is it to you what I want to buy?" Zuhura shouted.

"Okay, don't start screaming. This is not your house where you are used to shouting your head off." Sudi looked around nervously.

"If you don't give me some of the money you won on that bet last night, I will shout and tell people about this boy," Zuhura shouted. The two of them continued arguing as they walked briskly all the time. Ahmed was all out of breath by the time they arrived at Sudi and Zuhura's hut.

"My eye is on you, so don't try anything," Sudi said in a menacing voice.

"Yes, we have beings that you cannot see with your eyes. How do you think I was able to trick your rich friends into letting you come with me?" Zuhura shrilled. Ahmed felt a chill going down his spine. He had heard of *djinnis* that some people kept. Sudi and Zuhura looked exactly like the sort of people one would expect to be keeping *djinnis*.

"Go and fetch water from the well," Zuhura threw a bucket which hit him painfully in the shins.

"If you run away, you know what we will be sending after you, don't you?" she said in a threatening voice. Ahmed wondered if that was the same friendly woman that had offered to shelter him the previous evening. She looked so different—so evil!

What was worse was that he was required to fetch water from a well for the second time that day, and he was still feeling sore and torn from the first time he had done that. Besides he had not even been paid for that first time! It was so unfair. His footsteps felt heavier as he got closer to the well. Did Zuhura really have a *djinni,* or was it just another lie? He had been lied to so many times in the past few hours that he found it hard to believe anything grown-ups said. He looked at his blistered right hand. He thought of how the rope would feel on the fresh blisters. What more horrors did Sudi and Zuhura have in store for him when he went back to the house? He decided he did not want to wait and see. He glanced around swiftly. Zuhura had gone into the house and was loudly scolding her daughter Salma while her younger daughter cried piteously. It looked like all Zuhura ever did was shout and scold.

Sudi was nowhere to be seen. He had gone around the back of the house, probably to the outdoor bathroom. Ahmed walked calmly to the well. His heart was pounding so hard that it was as if it wanted to break out of his chest. When he reached the well, he put down the bucket and slowly started walking away from it. He expected any time to hear Zuhura's nightmarish voice calling him back. He clenched his fists and just walked further and further away, not daring to look behind him even once.

After he had gone past the hedge that surrounded the group of houses, one of which being Zuhura and Sudi's, he gained more courage and started walking faster. He darted down an alley and ran up another. Then he came to what looked like a mosque. It had a large leafy mango tree outside it that reminded Ahmed so much of the one back home. He walked—almost crawled because he was so exhausted—to the shade and sat down. He felt as if he was never going to be able to rise up again. His whole body ached so much. He was too tired to cry or even think. Before he knew it, he was fast asleep.

HALIMA

Suddenly, Ahmed was walking along a beach. The sand was so white that if he wasn't wearing his designer Calvin Klein sunglasses, he would have been totally blinded by it. He'd had them imported specially. He was rich and he had all the money he could ever need. The big house in the distance was his. His parents had bought it with the money he had won from the jackfruit.

Sheikha Abdallah was his girlfriend and had come to live with him because he had so much money. He had just been having his morning swim, and he was going to get a cool avocado smoothie. He was going to order one of the servants to make it for him. Then he would go and lie down in the deck chair and watch the tide coming in as he enjoyed the smoothie. Sheikha was going to sit down beside him, and they would joke and laugh the whole day. His parents let him do whatever he wanted to. His father was so nice that he always smiled at him and asked what he wanted to eat. His mother no longer had to sell *mahamri* and *kashata* and be worried all the time about money.

He hitched up the waist of his Bermuda shorts and adjusted his sunglasses on his nose. He slowly walked up the steps that led into the house from the beach, and a servant rushed to open the door for him. Just as he was about to enter, someone from inside the house splashed something cold onto his face. He spluttered and sniffed and woke up. Someone was laughing loudly at his antics. The very same someone who had splashed the cold water onto his face, and there were other people with him too. They were just boys, not much older than him.

"What are you doing in our territory?" the one who looked older asked. The look on his face made Ahmed quickly scramble onto his feet. He wildly thought that the liquid they had splashed onto his face was petrol and they were going to set him ablaze like in the video he had watched.

"Please don't burn me!" he cried out. The boys looked at each other uncertainly.

"Would we splash cold water all over you if we wanted to burn you?" the bigger boy asked. His relief was so great, Ahmed almost sobbed—even more when he realized that his body still ached abominably.

"Who are you?" one of the other boys asked. There were five of them, and they were all dressed in shabby, oily-looking clothes. Three of them had small bottles with a dark brown liquid in them which they sniffed from time to time. Ahmed had seen street children in his estate a number of times, but everyone avoided them as if they had a contagious disease.

"Ahmed," he answered, looking nervously from one to the other.

"Are you from Dharweish's gang?" another asked.

"Yes, they are the ones who put on the fancy clothes and go about as if they are better than us!' another boy said. Ahmed could feel the hostility from the boys as they stared down at him.

"No . . . no, please. I'm not from Dharweish's gang." He was just about to tell them that he was from Sudi's gang but on second thought changed his mind. Perhaps Sudi's gang was not the good one to belong to. Besides, were they thieves too, or was the gang they were talking about a different kind of gang?

"I . . . I don't have a gang," he said uncertainly.

"Oh, a newbie?" the older boy asked, his face softening as did the others. "You ran away from home, didn't you?" He squatted down as if he wanted to hear Ahmed's answer from closer up.

"Yes . . . uhhmm . . . no," Ahmed said uncertainly.

"Now, which is it, yes or no?" the boy asked. The rest of the group squatted or sat around him, eager to hear his story.

"Someone stole money from me, and now I can't go back home," Ahmed said sadly, the tears coming back into his eyes. The boys actually seemed quite sympathetic.

"Did they mug you?" the big boy asked, looking at Ahmed's blood-stained feet and hands.

"No, they . . . he said he was going to help me bet," Ahmed said in a little voice. To his disappointment, a teardrop slowly made its way from the corner of his left eye and down his cheek.

"Sportbet?" the big boy asked leaning forward

"Yes . . ." Ahmed dashed away the tears from his cheeks.

"Eh! People win a whole lot of money from that thing! If only I had a phone and I was a grown-up, I would try it over and over until Allah makes me win some millions!"

"Ali, stop dreaming," the big boy said. "You lose so much at Chege's, yet you keep trying!" The other boys laughed and jeered at Ali.

"Juma, you keep saying so, but someday I will win big, and then you will talk some other talk!" Ali said.

Now that they were all relaxed, Ahmed could think more clearly. Where was Chege's? Was it a place that children could bet, too? But then he had no money. Zuhura had dragged him from Mansur's before he could be paid. "Where is this Chege's?" he asked after clearing his throat nervously. It seemed to him that since leaving home the previous day, he had met more people than he had ever met in his entire life! He usually didn't talk to many people except his parents, sisters, neighbors, teachers, and some of his fellow pupils at school. He was becoming used to stranger people than he had ever known existed.

"You will know soon enough." Juma said loftily. It was as if they did not trust him much yet and they expected him to earn their trust. He wanted to ask how much money he had to have to be able to bet at Chege's, but he thought again that he shouldn't seem too eager. Another thing was that he felt awfully hungry. He had not had anything to eat since the breakfast very early that morning at Mansur's. Mariam had started preparing lunch just before Zuhura turned up. Ahmed felt quite angry just remembering that.

And his body, especially his head hurt so horribly. If he had any money, he would have gone and bought some painkillers. And where was he going to sleep? It was late in the afternoon. Perhaps he should just go back home. Maybe whatever his parents would do to him was not going to be as bad as all the things he was going through.

". . . here at the mosque . . ." Ahmed heard only the last part of what Juma was saying, but he figured out that he was saying they got their meals there at the mosque. As if on cue, the muezzin started making the call for the evening prayer. Ahmed stood up and started walking toward the mosque.

"Where are you going?" Juma asked.

"For prayers," Ahmed said. Some of the boys laughed.

Ahmed couldn't figure out what was so funny.

"Do you think they are going to allow a dirty *chokora* inside for prayers?" Juma asked.

"But I'm not a . . ." Ahmed started to say but couldn't bring himself to finish. He didn't want them to think that he was like one of Dharweish's gang, whoever they were, who thought they were better than everyone else. Instead he went back to the small circle the boys had formed and sadly sat down again.

"You will have to learn these things. You are no longer what you used be when you stayed with your parents," Juma explained patiently. Ahmed felt something lodge inside his throat.

"We will have to wait until they finish the prayers," Juma continued explaining. "Then the women will come with the donated food, and we will line up for it."

As they waited, Ahmed started thinking more about Chege's place that the boys had spoken about. Perhaps that was the place he was going to get the chance to earn the money he wanted so much, to be able to return to his parents. But then, it had gone beyond just returning the saree money to his mother. He also wanted to make some more for himself. He had never thought so much about making money, but it now seemed to him that was the only thing that he was thinking of.

"Is Chege's place far from here?" he timidly asked Juma.

"You want to make some money, don't you?" Juma answered with a question of his own. "Did the people who stole your money leave you with some to bet at Chege's with?"

Ahmed hung his head, but he was thinking all the time. There must be some jobs he could do to earn some money. After all, what did the street children do to survive? It seemed highly unlikely to him that they survived totally on what they were given at the mosque. "Is there any work I could do for the money?" he asked carefully. He didn't want to ask something that would make them laugh at him again or do other worse things to him.

"Oh, there are lots of things we do for money," Juma nodded his head in what Ahmed thought was a cheeky manner. He was certain Juma meant the kind of things that Sudi and his gang did. As if he had known what Ahmed was thinking, Juma explained some more.

"We sometimes wash cars, guard them, or help people to pack. But people don't trust us. We are dirty and poor! And we have to survive sometimes." That only confirmed Ahmed's fears. They did whatever they could to survive, and that perhaps included robbing other people!

He silently watched the people streaming into the mosque for the prayers, the women in their *hijabs* of many different colors, and most of them in black *buibuis*, the type that Ma Rahma always wore when going out. Most of the people who went in were men, some of them in ordinary shirts and trousers, but a lot of them in long white *kanzus* that dragged along the ground. For one moment he thought he had seen Ma Rahma, but it was just another woman.

He felt another pang of homesickness. He had to go back home soon. But every time he thought of going back, he also thought of the money he had lost. He was convinced that there was no way he could go back without the six thousand shillings for his mother. Whenever he thought of the six thousand, he also thought of how he could make some more money of his own while he was at it.

"Where exactly do you go to wash the cars," he asked again in a low voice. The evening was getting colder and he had started shivering. He had left Salma's jumper at Mansur's and the thin t-shirt he was putting on was no protection against the evening chill.

"Anywhere!" Juma replied sweeping his hand in a wide swath. "The whole world is our home, and we get whatever we do from any part of it." Ahmed didn't feel like his question had been answered, but he did not want to bother Juma anymore. It looked like he was going to have to make friends with that gang for his own survival, and to be able to get to Chege's, where he hoped he could win some money. Perhaps the six thousand and some more that he could keep.

The boys' interest seemed to be drawn towards the mosque as the worshipers started leaving after the prayers. There was a low hum of voices as people exchanged greetings and talked with each other with occasional laughter. It occurred to Ahmed that if he was at home, he would also be leaving the mosque with his dad and looking forward to a very nice meal that Ma Rahma would have prepared at that time. He felt the cold lump wedging in his throat once more.

He noticed that more and more street boys had silently come up to the mosque and were either waiting with silent expectation or talking among themselves in low tones. Some were whole families of street people, with women holding babies in their arms and one or two disabled men who crawled on the ground because they had no wheelchairs.

Ahmed could feel a mounting anxiety. Were they going to have to scramble for the food? Fortunately, they didn't have to. The street people seemed determined to be on their best behavior because the food meant a lot to them.

After he had a plate of rice and lentils, he went and sat down near Juma. He had already started warming up to the boy. As he gobbled down the unappetizing food, he looked around. There was the mother trying to feed a thin baby with some of the rice, but the sickly-looking baby did not seem to want any of it. He looked too young to be eating solid food anyway.

Then yet another bright idea struck Ahmed. Who washed the dishes for the women at the mosque? It must be so much work washing all those gigantic vats they served from and the posts they used to cook the food. Then there were the plastic plates that the street people used. Surely, they must need a lot of people to wash them?

"Who washes all these dishes?" Ahmed asked Juma.

"You seem to have so many questions, do you?" Juma drawled through a mouthful of rice and lentils.

"I just thought, maybe if I help with the dishes, they could pay me money to—" He was about to say "bet with," but changed his mind at the last minute.

"Hmmm . . ." Juma looked at him with amusement. "We don't know who washes the dishes. We just come for the meals and then leave. Those people just want to go to heaven and are using us as their ticket and it suits us just fine." Juma scraped the sides of his plate to get every scrap of food that he could. A ray of hope lit up in Ahmed's heart. There was hope after all! There was no way they were going to pay him six thousand shillings at the mosque, but at least they could pay him something to bet with.

"I think I will go in and ask for a job," Ahmed said as if he was asking for permission.

"That is your own problem." Juma shrugged his shoulders and stood up to return his plate. Ahmed was almost through with his too, and he quickly finished and followed Juma.

"So, who do I ask about the job," he asked in the politest way he could.

"I don't know," Juma said as he wiped his hands on the front of his grubby shirt. "Just one of those women, I guess."

Then he moved over and went to talk to the rest of his group as if he was determined to rid himself of the bothersome new friend. Ahmed stood and silently observed the serving ladies. Most of them were now swiftly moving around the mosque yard, collecting the plates that had rather ungratefully been left lying around on the ground by some of the street people they had just fed. The woman that had reminded Ahmed so much of Ma Rahma was coming towards where he was standing. She wanted to go collect some plates a little bit farther away.

"*Shikamoo*," Ahmed said softly. The lady looked startled, her eyes popping out as she answered the greeting after a while.

"Please, can I help with the dishes?" he asked still in a polite tone. The lady was not used to being talked to by the street people she fed, and it was definitely a new thing that one of them was offering to help with the dishes. She paused and took a closer look at Ahmed. She seemed to realize that he looked a bit different from the rest of the street people.

"What's your name?" she asked, moving even closer.

"Ahmed," he answered.

"Why aren't you at home? Do you live on the streets?" Ahmed wanted to tell her about his mother's lost money and everything he had been through, but then he thought that she might try to take him back home to his parents, and he did not want to go back until he had recovered the money.

"Uhhmm, I lost my parents," he said uncertainly. The lady probably thought he was being hesitant because he still found it painful to talk about his recently dead parents. She had already concluded that his parents had died.

"Oh, you poor child. Don't you have any relatives to take care of you?" she asked anxiously. "How long have you been on the streets?" Yesterday did not seem long enough to

Ahmed so he just told the lady that it was for a week. She put down the plates she had been holding and patted Ahmed on the head. It made him feel so guilty. He was not used to telling such lies.

"So, where do you spend the nights?" she asked. To Ahmed it seemed like she was on the brink of tears.

"Just outside," he answered because he had to give some sort of answer.

The lady gathered the dishes in one hand and led him into the mosque kitchen with the other, as if he was too weak unable to see where he was going and needed some sort of guidance. As she dramatically told the story about how the poor child had lost his parents and was now out in the streets, Ahmed wondered who it was she was talking about. He had hardly told her more than ten words, but she had woven a very colorful story of her own from them, spiced with more spices than Biti Rahma ever put in her *biryanis*. The rest of the ladies left everything they were doing and crowded around to see him from close up.

"God doesn't throw away his own!" he heard one of the women say, exactly what Zuhura had said the previous evening. It seemed like it had been so long ago!

"I will take him with me, poor creature," the lady, whom Ahmed had heard the ladies call Halima said. It was as if she was talking about a kitten.

"God will remember you on judgment day under the coconut tree." Ahmed had heard about the coconut tree where God would apparently reward people for good and punish them for bad deeds. That felt like cheating, making Halima think she was assisting an orphan, but he was too tired to worry about that. There were too many things to worry about at the same time.

"Wait for me in the inner court as we finish washing the dishes. You will not spend this night in the cold *inshallah*." Halima patted him on the head as she said that. The lady's kindness was kind of embarrassing to Ahmed, mostly since she got his story all wrong. But he was so tired that all he wanted was just somewhere to spend the night. The idea of sleeping out in the cold with Juma and his gang was quite scary, and so he just decided to play along. His mind went back to what the ladies were discussing.

"Inshallah! I won three thousand shillings, and I bet only one hundred!" One of the ladies was telling the others.

"Amiiiina! You too are into these things? Aren't they for children?" another asked.

"Is there old or young money?" Amina said. "It's not a sin. I don't think the holy book mentions Sportbet anywhere!" The other ladies burst into laughter.

"My sister's child, Nadia, got into trouble over those things. Now she has to hide out at my house," Halima clucked ruefully.

"My neighbor's son bet all the tuition fees his parents had struggled so hard to raise," Hafsa said. "This betting thing is satanic!"

"You see? In fact, it is not for the children, where would they get the money to bet with if they did not steal from their parents!" Amina said.

"I've heard of men betting their entire salaries, then they come home with nothing, and the women have to rush around to see how the children will eat and how the rent is going to be paid," another said.

"There is this lady who bet all the money in the *Mpesa* shop she worked in, hoping to double it and start a shop of her own!" Ahmed listened with a lot of interest. Had people always talked so much about betting? How come he had never noticed that before he started taking interest?

He was getting really drowsy before the women finished cleaning up at last. He was so glad that he did not have to help with the pile of dishes after all. His hands felt so sore and stiff from the blisters.

"Come Baba, let's go along home!" Halima urged him on. Ahmed quickly got onto his feet. Halima was carrying a plastic bag full of stuff, and he offered to carry it for her, which moved her so much. Her house was bigger than Zuhura's. There was young woman seated at a table writing something. She looked up when they entered.

"*Asaalam aleikum,*" she greeted Halima. When she asked who he was, Halima launched again into an even more interesting story than the one she told the women at the mosque. She definitely was a natural storyteller. The other lady was almost moved to tears.

"*Haya!* What are you going to do with him then?" she asked "Give him a place to sleep for tonight, then *inshallah*, if God allows us to see another day, we will see what will come with the day." She had forgotten to invite Ahmed to sit, so he slowly sat on the old brown sofa seat.

"Are you betting again?" Halima asked peering disapprovingly at the piece of paper that the younger woman was writing on.

"You never know when your lucky day comes," the young lady said, shrugging her shoulders.

"Haaah! Nadia, if only you didn't give up on a lot of other things," said Halima.

"Let me start the supper. What have you brought?" the young lady cut Halima short, probably because she did not want to discuss some things. Ahmed was paying rapt attention. He was already full from the meal he had at the mosque, but the spicy smells from the kitchen soon made him drool. That was the kind of cooking he was used to and the kind of smells that came from his mother's kitchen whenever she was cooking.

THEN YOU WILL LOVE ME!

Ahmed couldn't remember his body ever aching as much as it did when he woke up early in the morning. Halima had made a place for himself to sleep on the couch. He had fallen asleep almost as soon as he lay down. He woke up just once during the night when a drunk man came into the house and argued a little with Halima. She kept calling him Abu. When Ahmed woke up, the house was silent, except for some deep snoring that was coming from one of the rooms of the house. Back at his home, everyone would be up and about at that time of the morning. His father would already have woken him up for the morning prayers. He got up and spread the bed carefully. Then he drew the curtains. The sun was already rising. His hands felt so stiff. He winced with pain at every movement. His entire body was stiff and painful, perhaps from all the walking he had done in the past two days.

As he was opening the door to go outside, a young man came out of one of the rooms and stared at him as if he was used to seeing things that turned out to not be there at all. He rubbed his eyes, blinked rapidly, and looked again.

"Are . . . are you opening the door?" he finally asked hesitantly. Ahmed thought the man just wanted to hear him talk and to confirm that he was real.

"Yes," Ahmed answered. He wasn't sure of what else the young man expected him to answer.

"Who are you?" the young man asked.

"Ahmed." he could not think of anything else to say.

"Did you sleep inside here? They know you did?" He was becoming more awake with each passing minute and asking more questions as he did.

"Abu, stop troubling the visitor!" Halima called out from her bedroom.

"Oh. He was your visitor," Abu said with some relief. It was as if he thought Ahmed was some intruder. He walked over and helped him to open the door he was fidgeting with. The cold morning air felt so good. Ahmed sucked in a few breaths and felt better than he had in a while.

When he came out of the outdoor bathroom, he found Abu at the back of the house, looking at something on a folded piece of paper. He took a pinch of the substance and snorted it up his nose. Ahmed wondered if it was snuff. He had seen an old man who was their neighbor back home snorting snuff up his nostrils a number of times. Abu was so startled when he realized that Ahmed was looking at him.

"So, where did you say you come from?" he asked after he had hastily folded the substance up in the piece of paper and stuffed it back into his pocket.

"Kigogoni," Ahmed answered and immediately thought perhaps he should have said something else in case Abu decided to take him back there. But he had lost interest immediately after he got the answer. He sat on a bench that was leaning against the house and took out his phone.

"Might you be having something small . . . to you know . . ." He smiled in a kind of embarrassed manner. For a moment Ahmed had no idea what he was talking about. Was he asking him for some money? It would have been quite surprising if a grown-up had asked him for money a couple of days before, but in the past two days, Ahmed had seen and heard grown-ups do and say all manners of strange things.

"Something like . . .?" he asked uncertainly.

"A few coins . . . I lost some money last evening."

"Oh. I don't have any money," Ahmed said as he sat down beside him.

"I need to place a bet," Abu said thoughtfully. "Do you think you could convince my mother to give you some?" For a moment, Ahmed was lost until he realized that Halima was the mother that Abu was referring to.

"Are you pestering the visitor again, Abu?" Halima shouted from the house.

"Does everything I do have to be wrong?" Abu asked in a whiny voice.

"Ahmed baba, come for some water to wash your face with!" Halima called out, ignoring Abu's question. Ahmed rushed quickly to obey.

"That Abu is not a good person, baba," Halima said as she poured out some water for him in a basin. "He steals my things and goes to buy that evil powder with the money." Ahmed thought of the powder he had seen Hassan snort up his nostrils, and he was sure Halima was telling the truth.

"Just hate me for now. When I'm rich, then you will love me," Abu called out from the backyard. It sounded so funny that Ahmed found himself grinning.

"Aka! I don't blame you for laughing, baba. A grown-up like that with the brain of a child. May God protect you from such an end," Halima said.

"*Amiin*," Ahmed answered uncertainly. Just then, the young lady he had seen the previous day came excitedly from the house, waving her hands about with excitement.

"I got it! I got it!" she kept saying over and over. "What have you got?" Halima asked with surprise.

"I won!!!" she kept repeating over and over. The excitement brought Abu rushing in, but the sight of him made Nadia stop her excited dance.

"How much?" Abu asked

"How much did you tell me to win for you?" Nadia asked sarcastically.

"I'm just asking. Is it bad for your own brother to share your joy?" Abu asked in a sad note, as if to draw pity from Nadia.

"Ah-ah! Don't bring me your madness," Nadia said, going back into her room. Abu clicked his tongue and left the house.

CHAPTER 9

SOLD OFF

After breakfast, Ahmed wanted to help Halima around the home, but she insisted on pampering him all the time. He needed to do something. He wanted to earn some money to bet with. Abu drifted quietly away from the house while the rest of them were having breakfast, sending Halima into tirades about how he couldn't even eat a meal but went out to look for alcohol and "the evil powder" as soon as every day broke. Nadia had started taking an interest in Ahmed, asking him questions about his home and why he had gone out on the street. It had turned out that she had just won two thousand shillings on Sportbet after spending about the same amount betting. Ahmed chose to stick to the story about having lost his parents without going into details. He was only going to stay with them until he could get some money to bet with. Halima had found a pair of shorts and a t-shirt for him from among the bundles of clothes that he later learned she sold at the market.

"Don't you have any relatives, like anyone who could come

after you?' Nadia asked in a low voice. Halima had gone out to her business and asked Nadia to take care of Ahmed and make sure he was okay. Nadia was still very happy from the money she had won on Sportbet. She brought a glass of orange juice for him and some biscuits. Then she went into the house and started talking to someone on the phone. She seemed so discreet about it. Ahmed started getting worried. Perhaps she was up to some mischief.

"Will you escort me somewhere, Ahmed?" she asked when she came back into the sitting room. He thought she looked a bit nervous.

"Where?" he asked anxiously.

"Just to the shops." She had put on a very beautiful green *buibui* with glistening buttons at the front. She looked at the shorts Halima had given him thoughtfully, then rushed somewhere into one of the rooms and came back with another pair of trousers, which she quickly ironed and gave to him with some flip-flops.

"Here! Put this on," she instructed. Ahmed went behind the curtain and quickly put on the trousers. Somehow, he sensed that they were going to a much more important place than just the shops. Nadia's phone rang, and she glanced at him nervously before going into one of the other rooms to receive it.

"Hello, yes, I'm on the way, yes with one . . . not this time, yes, I know I let you down the other time . . . listen! Oh, okay." She hung up and clicked her tongue. Then she came back with a handbag and a bunch of keys.

"Let's go then!" she smiled warmly at Ahmed, but he was sensing that something was not quite right. He uncertainly went outside and she locked up the house after them. Walking was still a little painful to Ahmed, but the ointment that Halima had given him had dulled the pain a little. Nadia was walking quite fast, glancing around from time to time as if to see if anyone was following them.

As they stood by the roadside waiting for a tuk-tuk to town, she kept glancing at her tiny wristwatch anxiously. At some point, she actually jumped up and down a bit and wrung her hands as another text message came through on her phone. Ahmed watched her silently, wondering exactly what was eating her. At last, a tuk-tuk slowly came by and she frantically waved it down.

Ahmed had been to town a few times with his Biti Rahma or his dad but not to the part that Nadia took him. They went up one alley, across a busy street, then down yet another alley that was lined with old buildings with dirty yellow paint peeling off a lot of them. After glancing around for a while, she entered one of the old buildings. "Oh, here you are at last!" Someone said from a corner of the room. It was a bit dark, and after being outside in the bright sunshine, it took time for Ahmed's eyes to get used to the dim light inside the room. He slowly figured out that there were three men in the room. The one who had spoken was short and swarthy, with a bushy beard and the sharpest nose that Ahmed had ever seen.

"So, you've kept your promise for once, have you?" He started looking Ahmed over as if he was a goat at the market. It made him feel so uncomfortable. The other men also rose up from their seats and started examining Ahmed from close up.

"Do you think he is worth what you lost at the casino?" Khalid asked "You owe me big time, you know."

"Khalid, you know how grateful I am. Do you think this was easy?" Khalid seemed to consider her words. Ahmed's heart started beating once again. Now he was sure he was going to be taken through another scary experience by mysterious grown-ups. He wanted to ask what was going on and why they were all looking at him, but the words just wouldn't come. He started being even more afraid when it looked obvious that Nadia was going to leave him with the men.

"Where are you going?" he managed to ask, but his voice was just a whisper.

"I will be back. Just stay with Khalid while I go to the shops, okay?" Nadia bent and tweaked his cheeks as if to assure him. But somehow Ahmed felt like she was not going to come back at all.

"L . . . let me go with you," he said, realizing that his voice was trembling.

"No!" two of the men said in menacing voices as Nadia quickly went outside. Ahmed tried to dash out of the still-open door, but one of the men caught him by the back of his t-shirt and flung him into a corner of the room.

"Are you trying to run away already?" the man Nadia had called Khalid asked gruffly. Before Ahmed could reply, he gave him a stinging slap across his face. For a moment Ahmed was so stunned that he could not even cry out. He just stared wide-eyed at Khalid, and before he could even think, Khalid slapped him again, this time across his left cheek.

"Will you try to run away again?" he asked.

"No! Please don't hit me again!" Ahmed screamed, his voice breaking with fear. His thoughts were wild. What on earth was happening to him? Just a few hours ago, Halima and Nadia were being kind to him, giving him food and clothes and showing so much pity, and then all of a sudden Nadia left him with these terrible men who were hurting him! Perhaps God was punishing him for losing Ma Rahma's money. He wanted to ask what his mistake was, but he was afraid that the men would beat him some more if he talked again. He could feel the warm tears making their way down his cheeks.

"Get up!" Khalid barked at him, and he quickly scrambled to his feet. Khalid then caught him by the scruff of his neck and pushed him into another room. The force was so much that he fell onto some other people who were already in the room. The person he had fallen on hissed with pain and angrily pushed him away, but he just fell on top of someone else who pinched him hard and also pushed him away. Luckily, he fell on a bare place on the floor. He gingerly sat up, afraid of whatever was going to happen next. Slowly, his eyes got used to the dark room, and he saw that there were six other children sitting silently on the floor. Two or three of them had puffed up faces as if they had been beaten by someone. All of them looked very scared or just angry. None of them wanted to talk. Ahmed gingerly touched his face. It still stung where Khalid had struck him. He felt the side of his mouth with his tongue and tasted blood. He had, in the last two days, been hit and hurt more times than he had ever been in his life. He noticed that one of the boys was looking at him with pity. He didn't seem as angry as the others. Ahmed forced himself to smile at the boy, who looked down. But he looked up again, and then slowly inched closer to him.

"Hi," he whispered.

"Hello," Ahmed answered, trying to smile, although his mouth really hurt where Khalid had struck him.

"I'm Dauud," he whispered and Ahmed told him his name. The other boys started taking interest in their conversation.

"What is this place?" Ahmed asked.

"A warehouse. They are going to sell us to sailors to work on a ship." Dauud said.

"Sell us?" Ahmed was sure he had not heard correctly.

"Yes, as slaves. They will take us to work on some ship without pay, then dump us somewhere or sell us to some other ship afterwards." Ahmed had read about slave trade in history books, but he had never imagined that it still existed.

"I heard Khalid say that someone with a gambling debt was bringing a boy to settle her debts, then they brought you." Dauud divulged more. "You must be the one they were talking about."

Slowly, a picture of the situation he was in started forming in Ahmed's mind. Nadia had Khalid's debts that she had acquired through gambling, and she had given him to them as a payment! It started making sense to him. He was not going to be sold anywhere by anyone!

"So, what are we going to do?" he whispered anxiously. "What is there to do, pray?" Dauud asked.

"We cannot be sold to someone. It must be against the law!" his voice came out louder than he intended, and Dauud shushed him. The men were apparently very sharp-eared because they heard the door open and Khalid thrust his head into the room.

"Did someone talk?" he asked threateningly. None of the boys answered, so he just clicked his tongue, closed the door and went away. "We have to get out of here," Ahmed whispered desperately again. His heart had started pounding again, the way it did whenever he was very scared. The other boys started crowding around to listen to what he and Dauud were saying. They had given up all hope and had been so scared of the men. But when Ahmed and Dauud started talking, they suddenly had the courage to start hoping for a way out of their prison.

"When do you think they are going to sell us?" Ahmed asked. "I think tonight," one of the other boys replied.

"How long have you guys been around?" Ahmed asked.

"I found them here. I was brought yesterday," Dauud whispered back. The other five boys had been brought on different days in the course of the past week. As they gained courage, they huddled around and exchanged their stories in whispers. Most of them had been tricked before being kidnapped. The biggest of them had on the uniform with the badge of a secondary school Ahmed had heard about. He seemed moodier than the rest of the boys and was not very eager to talk about how he had come to be there.

"We have to come up with a plan," Dauud whispered.

"Yes," Ahmed nodded his head enthusiastically.

"But what?" one of the other boys asked. For a moment none of them could think of anything until, looking around, Ahmed saw the bucket in the corner that the boys used as a toilet.

"When do they bring you food?" he asked.

"Mostly at around three in the afternoon—lunch and supper all at once," someone said.

"What if we surprise whoever brings the food by throwing, you know . . . *that*," said Ahmed, indicating the bucket, "at them?"

Some of the boys giggled but caught themselves in time. Even the high schooler seemed to perk up and start to take more interest. Ahmed could feel the energy in the small room and the idea of throwing the waste into the face of whoever brought them food was a pretty exciting venture. But then something crossed Ahmed's mind. He remembered the story about belling the cat, which he had read in one of the books at school. Who was going to throw the bucket into the man's face? Fortunately, the high schooler eagerly agreed to do that.

"I hope it is going to be that Khalid," he hissed from between his teeth. "My ribs are still hurting where he kicked me yesterday."

"But what do we do when we get out?" Dauud asked, "I have never been to this part of town before!"

"The best thing is to stick together after we get out," the high schooler whispered. "Once we surprise the man, we should rush for the door, and then run as fast as we can, as far away from here as we can." They all nodded in agreement. With the new hope that they now had, the boys became more cheerful, exchanging stories of how they got into the room and even giggling with amusement at each other's jokes, especially whenever one of them had to use the bucket in the corner. As the evening drew near, they started getting more serious.

"I hope that bucket is not too heavy for you to carry and throw," Dauud asked. Some of the other boys giggled as the high schooler went over and tried to lift the bucket.

"I wish it was fuller, and I hope it is going to be Khalid who brings the food," said the high schooler. They listened carefully and realized that the men had stopped talking and moving around in the other room. They had probably left just one of them to guard the boys. Ahmed had wondered why they didn't just scream for help. But it turned out that was how Dauud had acquired the black eye and the bruises on his face. Khalid had threatened to kill anyone else who tried something like that.

Soon, they heard the voice of a woman and the clinking of metal dishes. They listened carefully and were sure that it was only one of the men that was in the other room. The high schooler's prayer had been answered because it happened to be Khalid. He took the bucket of waste and stood ready with it and the others stood right behind him, ready to go out as soon as he threw the waste.

Soon they heard the bolt of the door shoot back and the door being flung open. Khalid probably expected the boys to be huddled together in fear as they always were, as he had beaten them to submission. The bucket of waste in his face definitely was a great surprise to him. Quite a good deal of it must have gone into his mouth because he had just opened it, probably to bark some order at the boys. Before he could figure out what had just happened to him, the boys rushed out past him, with the high schooler giving Khalid a very hefty kick below his stomach before hitting him hard on the head with the empty bucket for good measure. The pain was too much for Khalid to even scream out. He just keeled over and curled up on the floor. The door that led outside was wide open and the boys rushed out. At first, some ran the opposite direction from others. Then, trying to correct the blunder, each of the groups ran the opposite direction before they paused and started going the same way. Ahmed ran as he had never run before. He didn't even know he could run so fast. In no time at all, he was at the head of the group. At some point, they came across a group of young men who were playing cards on a corner of the street, and the men too took off at top speed without knowing what they were running away from.

After a while, they saw some bushes along the lane, and Ahmed dashed around them and dropped to the ground. The rest of the boys followed suit and they all just lay there for a while panting heavily like hunting dogs. It was quite a while before any of them had the strength to speak at all. They looked at each other as if seeing each other for the first time. The high schooler looked younger than he had seemed in the dark room at Khalid's.

"Did you hit him on the head with the bucket?" Ahmed asked at last, breaking the ice. The boys guffawed as they remembered what they had seen the high schooler do. The moment made them forget for a while the situation they were in.

"I wish I had hit him until he died. See what he did to me last night?" he pulled back his shirt and showed them his bruised ribs. One of them seemed broken.

"Did he kidnap you from school?" Dauud asked the high schooler.

"Oh, that. No," the high schooler fidgeted nervously. Ahmed sensed that there was something the boy was not very proud to speak about.

"I was on the way to school," he said digging around with a sharp stick.

"Thn . . . he waylaid you?" Dauud pressed on.

"I lost my school fees *wewe,*" the high schooler answered quickly as if glad to get it out. Then probably thinking he had to explain so that he didn't seem as stupid and careless as to lose his school fees, he added, "It was a sure bet, I don't know how I lost."

"You bet your school fees away?" Ahmed asked.

"Look, the predictions were so clear," his voice trailed away. "And the odds . . ."

Ahmed didn't even know what the odds were; he just remembered that was what Zuberi had said he was going to check when he gave him the slip. It seemed so long ago, probably because he had been through so much and been to so many places.

"The odds were . . . look let's not talk about it okay?" The high schooler said in a whiny voice.

"I got conned out of some money too. Zuberi said he was going to play Sportbet for me, then he ran off with some money. Then Sudi wanted me to help him rob a house, but I didn't. Then Zuhura came for me . . ." Ahmed's voice rose higher and higher as everything he had been through came back to him.

"Hey, hey, cool down, bro." Dauud patted him on the shoulder. Ahmed realized that his fists were clenched. He didn't realize just how angry he was. What made him most angry was how Nadia had sold him off to pay her betting debts, just as if he was a goat or sheep.

They all started exchanging stories—Jim, Salim, Carlvo, Jamal, and the high schooler who Ahmad learned was called Omar. Most of them had been tricked in one way or another into Khalid's hands. But Carlvo had been a street boy for a few months after his mother died. They were sure that they were too far away for Khalid and his men to find them. The only problem was they had no idea here they were!

"This must be Kiganjoni," Omar said, glancing around. "Why do you think it is?" Dauud asked.

"Well, it just sounds nice, and I thought we might be there," Omar shrugged and started nibbling at his fingernails.

"You are not being helpful!" Dauud complained. "I have to get back to my aunt's house in Chanze. I know she will whip me raw, but at least I will have a place to sleep . . . and food." At the mention of food, the rest of the boys started speaking all at once.

"Maybe we should have waited to eat Khalid's food before we threw that filth into his face," Omar said with a serious face.

"Or we could have snatched the food and run away with it," Carlvo said sadly.

"Come *ooon*!" Ahmed laughed a little as he said that. "Who among us was thinking about food? We didn't even know whether we were going to get away!"

"The question remains . . . what are we going to do for food?" Omar asked.

"Is there a mosque nearby?" Ahmed asked.

"What do you want to do, pray for a miracle?" Omar snorted.

"They sometimes serve free food to people," Ahmed said with the assurance of experience.

"Oh yeah! My aunt sometimes helps with the cooking at the mosque near home!" Dauud said excitedly. Everyone agreed that it was a very bright idea. They came out from behind the bush and started walking along the road. The only problem was that they had stayed behind the bush past time and they had not heard any *muezzin* calling. They wandered through the streets and alleys, realizing from the signs above the shops that they were in Kilanze, which only Omar claimed to have ever heard of. They had come to take most of what he said with a grain of salt. They were not even sure whether he was joking or being serious a lot of the time.

Nightfall found them still wandering around like ghosts with no mosque in sight, the only thing they were sure of was that they were getting farther and farther away from Khalid and his men. They were sure that they were going in the opposite direction from the warehouse they had been imprisoned in. Then they came to a large eatery, and the supper crowd had just finished. Ahmed's mind thought again about the previous day and how volunteering to wash the dishes at the mosque had earned him a nice place to sleep.

"Do you think they will give us something to eat if we help them wash the dishes?" Ahmed asked. He had acquired quite a thing about dishes after the mountain of them at Mansur's.

"Who washes dishes? I've never washed dishes in my life." Omar shrugged his shoulders.

"We could try it. I'm very, *very* hungry!" Dauud said firmly.

A lady in a red *buibui* who seemed to be the owner of the food kiosk was in the process of scolding two girls in a shrill voice. When the boys approached, she looked so alarmed that she held one hand to her chest.

"*Mtumeee!*" She gasped dramatically, probably thinking they were going to rob her or worse. One of the girls quickly picked up the heavy pestle that had been leaning against the wall and raised it above her head.

"No, please, we mean no harm. We just need some help!" Dauud actually got onto his knees and held out his hands as he pleaded and quickly explained their plight and placed their request. Ahmed was too startled to even know what to think. Somehow, the lady, peering carefully at them through her round lenses, seemed to decide she could trust them.

"*Aka*! I guess we could use some help cleaning up. These ones are pretty much useless!" she said, her tone turning harsh as she glared at the very girl that was prepared to dash out their brains to protect her just a few minutes before. The leftover scraps were hardly enough to fill their aching bellies, but at least it was something. And what was better, the old lady let them spend the night at the ramshackle eating house and even gave them a dusty old canvas to sleep on. Aside from the mosquitoes and the knowledge that the coconut frond walls were no protection if anything or anyone decided to attack them, the boys were quite grateful for a place to spend the night.

PLACING A BET

The next morning found them huddled together and scratching mosquito bites. Ahmed couldn't believe the number of mosquitoes there must be in the world, if what had bitten them was just some of them! They were all stiff and in a totally foul mood. The lady arrived with her workers very early to prepare for the breakfast customers. She obviously didn't want them around. But she gave them some money to use as fare to wherever they came from.

"How much did she give you?" Omar asked Dauud, who the old lady had handed the money to on their behalf.

"Three hundred shillings." Dauud said after a quick count. "Enough for our breakfast?" Omar rubbed his hands together. "Wait a minute!" Ahmed said, "Why don't we bet with it, then we could get some more?"

"What!" Omar's voice broke as he almost shouted, "Were you listening at all when I told you about how I got into this mess in the first place?"

"That was you! I know I can hit it big at the first try!" Ahmed replied confidently.

"And how are you going to bet or get the money at all without any phone?" Omar asked

"You could bet in a cybercafé," Carlvo said uncertainly.

"Then if you win, the money will be sent to the cybercafé," Omar snorted.

"But there are other ways of betting. Let's look for a slot machine. I met some stree . . . uhhhmm . . . guys who bet using that!"

"By the way," Dauud scratched his chin thoughtfully.

"But I'm hungry, let's at least get some tea with some of the money," Omar said with a scowl that the others thought was quite threatening. He was bigger than the rest of them and could take all the money if he decided to. Besides, he was the one that had played the biggest role in their escape. After a cup of almost milkless tea and a transparent *chapatti* each, they wandered around for hours until they came to a shopping center and saw a group of people crowding around one shop's verandah. When they drew closer, they saw a small slot machine that each of the people was taking turns putting in coins and working certain levers, some cheering wildly as a string of coins streamed from a slot, and others trying to assault the machine as they lost.

"It has to be coins only?" Carlvo whispered.

"Didn't you know that?" Omar muttered. Apparently, he knew all those things too—he knew *everything*. He had asked for their change at the food *banda* to be given only in coins; ten and twenty-shilling coins. The people all seemed to be milling around without any order. Ahmed wondered how they were going to know when their turn to play came. There didn't seem to be any queue of any sort. He was so anxious to try his hand at the slot, he was sweating, his hands trembling with anxiety. He was so sure that he was going to win enough money from the slot machine to be able to buy a phone, and then they would be able to do Sportbet, on which people won hundreds of millions. In his mind, they were going to win big time! It seemed so easy, simple, and straightforward. The people milling around the machine were wasting his time. They didn't have the luck he was so sure he had; the way he had always found a way around every situation that had arisen was the proof that he was just plain lucky. The universe was prodding him towards Sportbet, so that he could win.

"Uhh, Omar, when is our turn going to come?" he asked nervously. Just then someone whispered something and the crowd just broke away from the slot machine. For a moment Ahmed thought they had sensed his eagerness to have a try and were giving way for him. By the time he realized that they were all taking to their heels and running away from something, it was too late for him. Someone caught up with him just after he had sprinted a few meters. He screamed and kicked out as hard as he could. There was no way someone else was going to take him captive - not again! One of his kicks caught the person that was holding him by the scruff in the shins and crotch, making him yell with pain . . . and he hit Ahmed hard on the head with what felt like a really big club.

When he came to, his body was aching in places other than the ones that had been aching before he was clubbed. He groaned and tried to turn to sit up, succeeding on his second try. His right eye was swollen almost shut, and his lips tasted of blood and felt like rubber. He was in a small crowded room, again! Peering from his good eye, he could see Omar and Carlvo among the people, mostly boys and young men, in the room. He painfully inched closer to Omar who didn't seem as injured as he was.

"What happened?" he painfully whispered through his swollen lips.

"Why did you kick the Town Council *askari* in the crotch?"

Omar asked "You want to commit suicide?" Slowly, Ahmed started realizing what had happened. The Council *askaris* had swooped down on the betting crowd, taking them completely by surprise. Ahmed and the rest of those who had not been lucky enough to get away were now in the cell, waiting to be taken to court.

CHAPTER 11

BEFORE THE COURT

The juvenile court was just a room with a desk at the front where the judge sat. There was a lady who read the names of the accused children and told them what they were accused of. Ahmed's dad sat with the parents of the other children who could be reached. At first, Ahmed had been too scared to call his father, but it seemed to him that he had hit a dead end. He had been so sure that his father was going to be raving mad. But the lady social worker had explained that his parents were probably beside themselves with worry, and he was definitely more important to them than the money he had lost.

His father looked so tired, with his face more creased than Ahmed remembered. What was more, he hugged him tightly, with tears in his eyes, which Ahmed had thought quite weird. The social worker had advised Ahmed and Omar to say that they were just spectators, watching the betting. The *askari* that Ahmed had kicked agreed to let it go after he had discussed something with Ahmed's father. Apparently, they were used to worse things than that in the course of their work.

Omar's parents had come too—all the way from Miritini. His mother cried throughout the court sitting, but his father, a gruff-faced older version of Omar, just sat there with a murderous look on his face. Ahmed feared so much for his newfound friend. He was quite sure that Omar was going to get it harder from his father than he was going to get it from his.

The judge read something lengthy from a piece of paper he had been scribbling on, but most of what he was saying was lost to Ahmed. He was so tired and sore all over, even his teeth and hair hurt. He just wanted to lie down and sleep forever. Later, they were taken back to another cell, and just after he had started to doze off, the door clanged open and some names, including his, were read out.

His father was silent throughout the journey back home on the *matatu*, until they got off at Kigogoni Center. When he stopped and looked Ahmed over.

"Should I take you to hospital? Are you alright?" he asked in the softest tone Ahmed had ever heard him talk in.

"No, I think I'm okay," Ahmed said hesitantly. "Zuberi tricked me. I lost the money. I'm so sorry." He could feel the tears coming again as he struggled to speak through his swollen lips.

"Your mother managed to get money for the women; it's all in the past now, but I hope you have learned your lesson," his father said in his usual voice. "Milk that is already spilt cannot be put back into the bottle," he added mysteriously as they turned onto the street that led to their home.

Ahmed thought ruefully that it was exactly what Zuhura had said at some point. He looked straight ahead as they passed the shop where Zuberi and his usual buddies were always playing *bao* on the verandah as if they had never left it, all the time Ahmed had been to so many places and through all sorts of things. You travel through hell and come back, and some people live their lives as if nothing unusual ever happened. Zuberi was not there, but the rest all pretended not to see him, as did Samir, who was watching the men play. Ahmed had a million things he wanted to say and do to Samir, but he followed his father silently. What had happened was now in the past; it was all spilt milk.– It was best to look straight ahead.

***

The kind of betting that was being done on the streets, like what he and the other boys had tried after they had escaped from the human trafficker's house, had been banned several months ago, but those responsible for enforcing the ban were negligent. That was what was reported in the news. The Sportbet Company had not been complying with the tax obligations.

"So much easy money, yet they do not pay what they should to the government? Ahmed's dad said, shaking his head with wonderment.

To Ahmed's surprise, his father had not been as angry as he had expected him to be. He just looked exhausted. Ahmed wondered what had happened, and then his mother had explained the anxiety they had gone through when he had disappeared.

"Our first thought was that something must have happened to you—something bad," she had explained. That had been the last thing on Ahmed's mind. The fact that they would worry themselves sick about what had happened to him. He had assumed that they had somehow been aware that he had lost the money he had been given and that it was the only reason that he could not come home that evening.

After asking around, one of the men at the shop had told Ahmed's father about his conversation with Zuberi. None of them had wanted to divulge that they knew exactly what had happened.

"But they were there all the time! They witnessed everything that went on between Zuberi and me!" Ahmed's voice had risen when Ma Rahma had told him about it.

"Yes, but who would want to get involved in things that are none of their business?" Ma Rahma had shrugged her shoulders. The good thing, though, was that Zuberi had been taken into a rehabilitation center after that. His brother had come over for him when he had heard that Zuberi might have gotten himself into some kind of trouble that was related to drugs. He had been on and off drugs, until he had left his hometown some months earlier.

"And what about Samir?" Ahmed felt a rush of anger when he mentioned his buddy's name—ex-buddy actually. He most definitely was not going to have anything else to do with that rascal. That was the last time that Samir was going to get him into trouble, ever. Then he remembered that it was what he promised himself whenever Samir got him into trouble, but it still happened again and again. Perhaps he could just avoid Samir altogether. Samir had denied even talking to Ahmed that evening and Samir's parents had believed him. Maybe they were just doing what they could in order to keep their son out of trouble. Ma Rahma said that she hoped for Samir's sake that they did give him a good talking to afterwards.

"Maybe they just did not want to talk to him in public." She shrugged.

After his father had not found any useful information from the men at the shop or from Samir, he had gone straight to the police. He did not want to talk much about it, Ahmed soon figured out. The officers at the police department did not seem too eager to help. Perhaps he had expected them to quickly get a police car with blaring sirens and flashing lights and begin searching for Ahmed.

"But they said that you have to be missing for at least forty-eight hours for them to be able to record you as a missing person," Ma Rahma said as if it was the stupidest thing she had heard in all her life. "Forty-eight hours they said!" she exclaimed, rolling her eyes and raising her hands to the heavens. "Here is a desperate parent trying to find his lost son, and they tell him that he cannot be lost, until he can't be seen for two days!" After his father had told her what he had been told at the police station, she decided to go there herself. "You know, your father sometimes gets a bit soft with people." She shrugged and fidgeted with some embarrassment as she told Ahmed that, "sometimes people have to be told things exactly the way they are." Apparently, she had raised quite a rumpus at the police station. They had threatened to lock her up in a cell if she did not leave immediately. They even called a female officer to push her into a cell, but then she had quickly come back to her senses and decided that it was better, after all, to keep herself on the outside if she was going to be able to help her son in any way. Even she knew when she had to give up.

"I shouted until I lost my voice," she said. Actually, her voice was still a bit hoarse—hoarser than it usually was, Ahmed noted at the time. Looking at her as she remembered and narrated to him what had happened, he also noticed that there were lines around her mouth that he had never noticed before. Perhaps worrying about him had made her a little older than she really was. He felt so sorry. Then she thought about his cousin Zaruni's wedding. Did his disappearance ruin everything?

"And Zaruni's wedding?" he asked sadly, dreading what he was sure she was going to tell him.

"Oh, it went on as it had been planned, but without me." He noticed that her mouth tightened when she said that. She had managed to borrow money to pay for the sarees and the women had been able to wear the dresses they had chosen to wear to the wedding. He felt amused that the wedding had gone on without Ma Rahma's help after all. Perhaps his mum finally realized that she was not the one that was holding up the sky, and it wouldn't fall down and crush everyone if she relaxed and let other people do some things. It was at that point that Ahmed's dad had come into the room.

"You realize that you will have to work to repay the money you lost, don't you?' he said in a voice that sounded more like the one that Ahmed was used to. Ahmed felt a rush of fear. Was he going to have to leave school and do some horrible work like at construction sites, carrying mortar and bricks? But then he really deserved some kind of punishment for what he had done to his parents. He sighed and looked down.

"Yes, I guess so."

"What got into you anyway?" his father asked, recovering more of his usual voice.

"It is that boy, that Samir!" Ma Rahma jumped to Ahmed's defense, raising her voice.

"There you go defending him again!" Ahmed's dad spread out his palms.

"No, I am just saying the truth," Ma Rahma said as she gathered up her dress around her and stood up to leave.

"Anyway," Ahmed's dad continued, "every day after school, you will go up the street to Langoni, where my cousin Musa has his café. You will help him by waiting tables and doing any other work that he needs done, until the money is repaid."

Ahmed's spirits rose as soon as he realized that he was not going to have to leave school after all. Then as soon as his dad mentioned his cousin in Langoni, his spirits sank again. Uncle Musa was even stricter than his dad. It definitely was not going to be easy working for him. If it had to be done, though, then that was how it was going to be.

Perhaps it was high time that he had to learn to stand on his own two feet and earn his own money. The last few days had taught him that there was no easy money without some kind of trouble attached to it. Good money only came down one route: hard work. He had also learned just how much his parents cared—especially his dad, even if it did not seem that way a lot of the time. Thrust suddenly out of the warmth and comfort of the home he was used to, he had realized that people lead much tougher lives. His parents had actually cushioned him from a lot of what other children had to go through elsewhere.

Most of all, he now knew that not all parents were as trustworthy as his parents and most of the other grown-ups he knew. He could not trust everyone, just because they were grown-ups.

THE END

GLOSSARY

Aka!	Exclamation of surprise or outrage, like WOW
Alhamdulillah	Praise God/thank God
Asaalam aleikum	Greeting; peace be upon you
Askari	Policeman/guard
Baba	Daddy; also used as an endearment for young boys
Banda	Food kiosk
Bao	A board game usually played by grown men
Bhajia	Snack made with mashed potatoes, onions, and spices; then dipped in egg and deep-fried
Biryani	Spicy rice dish
Buibui	Long outfit, usually black, that Islamic women and girls wear over their everyday outfits when going out of their houses
Duka	Canteens or small shops
Halua	A popular sweet/condiment
Haya	Okay
Hijab	A headcloth won by Islamic women; sometimes very colorful
Inshallah	God willing

Kanzu	Long (usually ankle-length) outfits won by men and boys; white ones are usually worn for prayer and on other special occasions
Leso	Colorful cotton wrappers with sayings inscribed on them
Mahamri	Type of bun made from wheat flour, coconut milk, and spices; deep-fried
Mandazi	Buns/doughnuts
Marahaba	Response to *shikamoo* (may it be well)
Maskiini/maskini	Poor thing
Matatu	Public service vehicles/taxis; usually vans
Mkeka	Mat woven from palm fronds or straw; often used for Islamic prayer
Mpesa	A mobile money transfer service
Mtume! (prophet)	Often used as an exclamation in moments of fear, anxiety, or pain
Saree	Matching long, colorful flowing silk dresses and headscarves; usually worn by women and girls for special occasions
Shikamoo	Greetings of a young person to their elder (I touch your feet)
Sportbet	Fictional betting firm that facilitates betting on the outcome of soccer games from around the world
Taarab	Slow songs usually accompanied by wind instruments and drums
Tuk-tuk	A three wheeled, canopied, motorized vehicle mostly used for public transport
Ukwaju	Tangy condiment made from the seeds of the baobab tree
Wifi	Sister-in-law
Ya rabbi	Goodness gracious!